HOME WRECKER

Part One of the Loyalty Lock Series

JANUARY 1, 2016

SELF PUBLISHED

Tennessee

For those who struggle to overcome adversities of every kind. "We are afflicted in every way, but not crushed; perplexed, but not driven to despair; persecuted, but not forsaken; struck down, but not destroyed…"

1 Corinthians 4:8-9

Chapter 1

The town could be likened to the fourth leg of a table. On its own, it didn't hold any real value, but when combined with three of the other nearby towns, it became significant enough to bear the weight of a few national retailers and some decent restaurants. Situated in the eastern part of Tennessee, tucked into the rolling hills and hugged by rippling creeks, Cleveland was Mary's home. If the south was the Bible belt, this town was the brass buckle. It held dozens of churches. Crosses hoisted high upon steeples could be seen all over. People who loved Cleveland affectionately referred to it as "God's Country," while the less adoring folks said it was made of a sinking sand that wouldn't let you loose once you lived there. It was no matter to Mary, because to her, it was simply home sweet home.

Mary Montgomery and her husband, Philip, had been high-school sweethearts. Their lives could have been ripped from the pages of a fairy tale. The six-foot-two-inch star quarterback had been in love with Mary since grade school, and as soon as his sixteenth birthday approached, he gained permission from his parents to date. He had never looked back. For Philip, it had always been and would always be Mary.

Twenty years of marriage had lavished good fortune upon the two. On a sprawling piece of land brimming with mature cedar trees sat their dream home. In the early 1900s, it had been called a mansion, but by modern standards, it was simply an old house on Ocoee Street. Mary and Philip had spent the better part of seventeen years refurbishing each room. Their three children had never lived anywhere else. Each had been brought home from the hospital and placed into the same antique cradle in the nursery next to the master bedroom suite.

William, now sixteen, was the first. Very much like his father, Wills was quick-witted, athletic, and handsome. Five years passed before his younger sister, Tatum, entered the world. Unlike Mary, who was feminine and soft, "Tate" was a tomboy who wanted to be just like her big brother. To her, he was the most magnificent human being on the planet. From day one, she adored her Wills.

Nothing, however, had prepared the family for the joy that arrived on Philip and Mary's fifteenth wedding anniversary. The youngest Montgomery arrived two weeks early by a cesarean section, very much unlike her brother and sister, who had both been delivered by natural childbirth. When the doctor turned to hand the five-pound-one-ounce bundle to the nurse, Philip recalled the nurse's expression. Something didn't seem quite right with the way she looked at the baby. He almost questioned her out loud, on the spot. But instead, he turned to Mary, who was smiling at him.

"We did it, Chief!" she spoke. His heart always melted when she called him Chief. On the first day of their marriage, she had named him the Chief Marriage Officer. Over time, the name "Chief" had stuck. Her voice was tired; she had been put through such an ordeal prior to the emergency surgery when the labor caused the baby's heart rate to plummet. At one point, they thought they might lose their daughter. He wondered how his wife remained so calm even in the midst of such a great storm.

Later that evening, Philip had climbed up into the hospital bed next to Mary as the two inspected baby Charity. The big, strong athlete who had become a successful business owner eventually broke down and sobbed while Mary held both him and Charity close to her: "We are going to be fine, perfectly fine. I've always heard it said that God gives special babies to special families. And we, Philip Montgomery, have a wonderful family to offer Miss Charity."

And that was how the youngest daughter, who was born with the extra chromosome, came to be known in town as "Miss Charity."

By five years of age, Miss Charity had positioned herself as the one at the center of the family. A thick pair of glasses were a constant reminder of her poor vision, while a scar on her chest told the story of a serious heart defect. Still nonverbal, the big-brown-eyed girl in pigtails could say one word: "Da-Da." If Mary was Philip's universe, Miss Charity was his brightest star. Wills and Tate adored her too. She could be found most afternoons on top of

Will's broad shoulders, giggling with abandon as he tromped through the house acting like a horse carrying its favorite cowgirl. And in the evening, she snuggled in Tate's bed, listening to her read stories of princesses who lived in faraway places. While Tate didn't enjoy princess stories, she knew her little sister did. So at night, the eleven-year-old tomboy with skinned knees would place a crown upon her sister's head, swaddle a Cinderella doll beneath her tiny little arm, and read until she heard a soft purr escaping from a tiny, rosebud-shaped mouth. Miss Charity was the colorful bow that completed the Montgomery family package. Mary was living the life she'd always dreamed of.

It was no wonder the enemy sought to destroy their lives. After all, scripture warns he comes to steal, kill, and destroy. What was most tragic, though, was that they never saw it coming. When the devil slunk in like a thief in the night, he stole everything from the family. Well, almost everything. And unbeknownst to Philip and Mary, he had been at work for many years. In fact, it all began on Wills's first day of eighth grade when a boy named Crew Cutless walked onto the campus of Ocoee Middle School like he owned the place.

The following is their story.

Chapter 2

"So, Wills, are you ready for the big game tomorrow night?" Mary spoke over Miss Charity, who was banging the keys of the baby grand piano in the front room. The sound echoed, bouncing off the high ceilings before rushing through the house in a tidal wave of noise. She continued: "Bradley versus Cleveland football...it doesn't get much bigger than that in this town."

His mother continued to stir the last of the milk into the bowl of mashed potatoes, attempting to ignore the sound coming from the front room. Wills wondered how she managed to form any thought with all the commotion in the house. Just before he could answer, the house became still and quiet.

"Hold that thought!" Mary said, raising her finger as she rushed into the front room.

A few seconds later: "Oh, Wills, come quick. You are not going to want to miss this."

He'd been checking his text messages but quickly put his phone down on the kitchen counter. When he rounded the corner, he pulled up fast and stopped right next to his mother. His shoulders stood a whole ten inches above Mary's, and they were nearly twice as broad. In unison, the two looked at each other and giggled out loud. Miss Charity had removed every stitch of clothing except for the big, pink bow that remained on top of her head. Seated on the piano bench, the five-year-old (who was the size of a three-year-old) turned to give them a sheepish glance. Even in her complete silence, she communicated her thoughts with an expression that stated: "Uh-oh, I've been caught by the clothing police again."

"How in the world does she get her clothes off so fast?" Mary asked, shaking her head at the sight of her little girl's pants, shirt, socks, and shoes strewn around the room. "The therapist calls it sensory issues...but—"

Wills interrupted with a dreadfully gut-busting imitation of Sherlock Holmes: "Like I've tried to tell you before, Mrs. Montgomery, this has nothing to do with sensory issues. Miss Charity is making a bold statement." Wills then put his hand up to his cover his mouth, leaned over toward Mary, and acted like he was telling his mother a guarded secret that held the answer to all of her troubles: "Your youngest offspring wants to be a nudist, and I fear you might as well accept it." Wills gave his mom a shrug with his best smirk.

"Well, fat chance of that ever happening, Miss Charity," Mary scolded as she reached down to pick up the shirt, which had landed on a chair after being tossed aside by the five-year-old pianist. "Look at you seated there acting as if playing the piano in the nude is a completely normal thing to do. You have to wear clothes, girly girl!"

As Mary came closer to Miss Charity, the little girl realized she was going to be forced to be restricted in clothes again. In response, she scooted off the piano bench in a flash and streaked out of the room as fast as her legs would carry her.

"Get her!" Mary shouted to Wills.

But Wills was no help. He had taken one look at Miss Charity's plump little fanny darting out of the room and had fallen onto the floor in a heap of laughter: "Look at her go, Mom! Miss Charity is standing up for Adam and Eve and is bringing nudity back!"

Wills's outburst of laughter struck a funny chord with Mary, so she broke out into a roar of laughter with him. The two found themselves rolling on the floor, holding their stomachs, while laughing hysterically: "I can hear her feet pounding on the wood floors...she's still streaking through the house...making her statement!"

Wills and Mary laughed until tears streamed down their faces. Nearly two minutes passed before they realized the house had become quiet once again. Together they shrieked: "The mashed potatoes!"

But they were too late. When they ran into the kitchen, their fears were welcomed with a startling reality. Sitting in the middle of the floor, with a bowl between her legs, was Miss Charity. In a rush to seize the opportunity, she had not even considered a spoon. Instead, she had grabbed the big bowl and used her fingers to dig into the warm, freshly mashed potatoes. The proof was all over her fingers, her face, and the kitchen floor.

Wills once again borrowed the voice of Sherlock Holmes: "I say, Mrs. Montgomery, it looks like your mystery has been solved. The mashed potatoes were not eaten by the butler, by Professor Plum, or by Mrs. Peacock...but by the little nudist who plays your piano."

Wills and Mary continued to chuckle as they cleaned up the mess and dressed Miss Charity.

"Clothes on," Mary insisted as she forced the final shoe onto the foot of the now completely dressed five-year-old.

"I think she believes you're mad at her," muttered Wills while patting his sister on the head as if she were a cute puppy.

Miss Charity couldn't speak, but she understood everything. Taking her brother's cue, she offered Mary a puppy-dog pouty face. And it worked. It always worked.

"Oh, you two have me so well trained. I only wish I could train the both of you!"

Mary pulled them close and hugged them tight. "Why, oh why, did God have to make you both so completely irresistible?"

Wills watched as Miss Charity's face lit up like the sun. In nothing flat, he scooped her up onto his shoulders with a cheer: "Well, I can no longer resist this little cowgirl, who must be eager to ride her favorite pony!"

The two bounded out the door and into the backyard, while Mary returned to the kitchen to get dinner together. Moments later, the door swung open to reveal a thundering Tate, pulling Mary's mother, GiGi, behind her. She breezed through the house and straight out the door to join her brother and sister in the backyard, barely noticing her mom in the kitchen and leaving GiGi behind to fend for herself.

"So, GiGi, did you have any success getting our tomboy a new pair of sneakers?" asked Mary.

"Almost, but we ran out of time. She had me in such a rush to get her home, I nearly broke out in hives. Every few minutes she felt she had to remind me: 'Thursday is a short football practice, so Wills will be home early'...she was like a constant drip in the bathroom sink, reminding me every few seconds. The only way I could turn her off was to bring her home."

Mary replied: "I don't know if I'll ever get her out of those 'lucky' shoes. She says she is playing basketball better than she's ever played before."

"Well, those 'lucky' shoes stink. I have never smelled anything quite so ferocious in all my life. Perhaps we could throw them away and suggest they've gone missing."

Mary pulled the meatloaf from the oven and sat it on the counter. "Thanks to Miss Charity, we'll be having meatloaf sandwiches this evening instead of meatloaf and mashed potatoes."

"Dare I ask what happened?"

"No, don't dare. And don't even think of throwing away Tate's lucky shoes. She won't be a little girl much longer, so let's allow her to enjoy the time she has left...ferocious smells and all." Mary gave her mom a smile and a wink.

"Well, as much as I would like to have one of your meatloaf sandwiches, I'm meeting your dad out for dinner this evening and better be going." GiGi pulled the powder from her brand-new Coach purse and applied it generously to her nose and cheeks. "Lord, Mary, I think I broke a sweat tearing out of the shoe store with Tate today. Your father, and everyone else in town, is going to think I'm a complete mess."

Mary grinned, watching her mother straighten the size 6 pair of Gap blue jeans that fit her perfectly. One thing was certain about GiGi: she was not going to let age get the best of her.

"You couldn't be a complete mess if you tried. And I don't have enough meatloaf for you and Dad anyway. One of your favorite people, the infamous Crew Cutless, is coming for dinner this evening. His parents are out of town, so he'll be spending the night with us too. He and Wills are so excited about the game tomorrow night; I don't know if they'll get a wink of sleep."

"You better make sure they do. The Bradley Bears will not be victorious without their star quarterback and receiver. See you tomorrow night, honey. I'll be the one wearing black and gold."

And with a quick hug, GiGi was out the door.

Later that night, as the teenage boys sat playing Madden 25 on the Xbox, the world seemed perfect to Wills. His body was tingling with anticipation about the big game, and his heart was full of love for family and friends. But youth and innocence can't linger forever. The Sherlock Holmes impersonator had no idea of the plans Crew was brewing in his mind for the next evening.

Chapter 3

Wednesday morning was cool and damp when Philip found Preacher Walker making his routine prayer walk around Bradley High School.

"Philip, what a surprise!" he said, reaching out a hand to give a pat on Philip's back. "I didn't get a chance to catch up with you after church on Sunday. I'm so happy to see ya."

"When I called your house this morning, Jeannie said I could find you here. I felt like I needed to join you today in your prayer walk, if that's OK."

"Of course it's OK. I can use the company." The pastor with the gentle soul began to walk again, motioning for Philip to join him. "I usually walk around the school three or four times, just allowin' the Spirit to direct me in how to pray." Giving Philip a big smile, along with a thump of his chest, he continued: "I don't pray out loud, just quiet and still...right here...in my heart."

Preacher Walker, seventy years young, small in stature, and sporting a shock of snow-white hair, walked side by side with Philip as they prayed. They both prayed for the students in the school, but the kind old pastor also prayed for his buddy who had joined him. After three times around, he stopped.

"I sure am hungry. How about we head down to the Rebel and fetch us a biscuit and gravy?"

Philip didn't even have to think about it. "Sounds good to me. I'll drive."

The Rebel Drive-In restaurant, with its signature neon sign, was a staple in the small town. In operation for nearly fifty years, it had been the first in the region to offer the electronic car-side ordering system. Philip had hated it when the burger joint finally gave in and did away with the system several years prior, because he had fond memories of climbing into his father's lap as a boy to push the red button on the box and call in the order. One thing had never changed: the place still had the best sausage gravy on the planet.

In less than five minutes, the two found themselves seated in a booth by the window drinking perfectly brewed coffee. Silence didn't bother the wise man of God, so he decided he'd keep his mouth zipped and allow Philip to talk about what was on his mind whenever he was ready. It didn't take long.

"So, I guess you've already figured out I met you at the school today because I needed some advice."

"Yep, I figured as much," was the preacher's simple reply.

"It's hard to believe you married Mary and me twenty years ago. You and Jeannie have been with us through every stage of life. Heck, you've been Mary's pastor since she was a little girl. I just thought you'd be the best person to talk to."

Philip picked up the coffee mug, took a sip, and paused to look out the window. Meanwhile, the beloved friend seated across from him said nothing but prayed silently in his heart: "Lord, please give Philip the courage to share what's botherin' him, and help me to be real good at listenin' to what he's got to say."

The younger man turned back to face the one who had become very much like a second father to him. "It's Wills. I think something is going on with our Wills."

The waitress stopped at the table to deliver the steaming-hot biscuits dripping in gravy. After she returned to refill the coffee cups, Philip thanked her and held his mug up to make her job a little easier. Preacher Walker, though, never took his eyes from Philip.

As the waitress poured the coffee, the southern minister was overwhelmed with a sense of dread. His heart started pounding. It was as if the Spirit of God was warning him that something was very wrong. The Rebel was full of people, and not one of them knew the silent prayers being uttered by the man seated in the brown vinyl booth by the window: *Lord, not Wills. I was at the hospital the day that boy was born. Your hand is upon that boy; I've seen it clear as day. He's like the grandson I never had, Lord. You've got a tremendous plan for him...*

The waitress walked away, and Philip's eyes returned to his pastor who was now looking back at him with genuine concern. Philip continued: "You know we've never had a moment of trouble from Wills. He's almost been a perfect child, as strange as that might sound." He paused a few seconds to fight back emotions. "You've known him his whole life, so you know what I'm trying to say. I think something might have happened after Friday night's game."

Preacher Walker began eating his biscuits, giving Philip the obvious go-ahead to continue talking.

"As you've probably heard, Wills and Crew had the game of their lives Friday night against Cleveland. It was like magic happened between the two. Every pass Wills threw was caught by Crew. It was an incredible thing to see. Wills left the game with Crew and a bunch of guys. He ended up spending the night out and spent Saturday night out too. Mary and I didn't think anything of it, because we knew the football players wanted to celebrate...and they deserved a big celebration. But when Wills came home on Sunday, he wasn't happy. He was distant and seemed upset or angry. He went up to his room and stayed there all day. Same story on Monday and Tuesday. He's gone to school, stayed for football practice, but then comes home and goes straight to his room...doesn't even talk to us. We keep trying to talk to him, but he turns us away saying nothing is wrong, that he just wants to be alone. Mary and I are getting worried and don't know what to do."

Philip picked up his fork for the first time. He jabbed a piece of his biscuit, stirred it into the gravy, and took a bite. Preacher Walker knew it was now his turn to speak. He pushed his plate away, wiped his mouth, and took a final sip of coffee. In his mind, he was again praying: *Lord, give me wisdom. Help me not be blinded by my love for this family so that I might speak truth.*

His cup clanked against the saucer as he sat it down. He then cleared his throat and began: "Philip, I love your family with my whole heart. I really do. The bunch of you are like my own kids and grandkids, so this is hard for me. I can't help but find it ironic that we're sittin' here in a restaurant called 'The Rebel.' I wonder if Wills hasn't come face-to-face with the inner rebel that's in all of us. As you know, in one of our favorite books, the book of Romans, Paul even talked about how he struggled with doin' things he didn't want to do. We've all sinned and fallen short. Even Wills. I agree with you and Mary. Sounds like something's up. But let's not panic just yet. Instead, keep on doin' what yer doin'. Try to talk to him, plan some family activities, love him, and above all, stay on your knees. You can rest assured I'm gonna be on my knees. In fact, son, let's pray right now."

Waitresses buzzed about balancing trays loaded with food...people of all ages laughed and carried on conversations around them...the sound of '50s music exploded through the sound system...but the two men of God were oblivious to it all. They reached across the table and grasped tightly to one another. One man's hands were worn with age, the other's still vibrant and strong. With their heads bowed, they took turns praying. This time they prayed out loud. Tears dripped from their eyes and landed on the laminate tabletop like droplets of rain. Neither cared. Love for Wills poured from their souls, and the unseen angels surrounding them heard every word.

Chapter 4

Several days passed with no change in Wills's conduct. If anything, he had become more distant and despondent. Miss Charity's behavior shifted drastically in response to her big brother pulling away from her. Unable to speak, she was showing her frustration by throwing things, having frequent screaming tantrums, and banging her head on the floor. And Tate was starting to ask lots of questions: "What's wrong with him? Is he mad at me?" Mary, in turn, became desperate to seek a solution before her whole family went to pieces. She decided to ask her sister and mother for some advice.

"Thanks for stopping by for lunch today. Tate is at her homeschool tutorial group for the next couple of hours, and Miss Charity is playing at the neighbor's house, so we have some time to deal with an issue before I have to pick them up. If you don't mind, I'm going to get right to it," Mary said while leading her mom and sister to the dining-room buffet, where she had laid out their sandwich fixings, fruit, and sweet tea.

They each fixed a plate and sat down before another word was spoken. Mary's sister, Viv, spoke first: "So, Mom has filled me in on what's going on with Wills...the strange behavior...and since you want to get right to it, we both have a theory. You tell her, Mom."

GiGi, who never ducked an opportunity to give her opinion, sat up straight, raised her chin, and said matter-of-factly: "He's having sex. I'm sorry to say it, Mary, but you surely know boys lose their ever-lovin' minds whenever a girl comes along and steals their virginity. If you find out who the little she-devil is, you'll fix this problem straight away." Then GiGi promptly took a bite of her chicken-salad sandwich and began to chew.

Mary, aghast, turned to look at Viv, who bluntly punctuated the point with a mouth full of her own sandwich: "What Mom said."

"Really?" Their words sank into Mary's mind before rolling around in her belly like a bunch of wild bumblebees fighting over nectar in a honeysuckle bush. "I just don't see it. We've raised him to save himself for marriage, and he has always said that's what he would do. Besides that, he isn't even dating anyone."

"Hello? Anyone at home, Mary?" Knocking on the table as if it were a door, GiGi replied to Mary with way more than a hint of sarcasm while shaking her head with disgust. "Honestly, I raised you to be more with it. Wake up and listen to me tell you about 'Sin Land'! These kids today don't have to date to have sex; they just have sex to have sex. Don't you ever watch *Dr. Phil*?"

"Mother," Viv replied, "Mary has lived in 'My Life Is Perfect Town' for so long, she hasn't even allowed her big toe to touch 'Sin Land'...she doesn't speak the language and probably doesn't even understand what you're saying. Let me try to get through to her."

And then with a booming voice, speaking very slowly, Viv continued: "Maaarrrryyy...Wiiillllsss isss haaavvviiinnnngg seeexxxx."

GiGi cut in while biting off a piece of strawberry: "Either that or he's hooked on porno. You know, porno is the big thing now on the Internet. Naked people everywhere at your fingertips."

"If this is true, what on earth will I do?" Mary asked, while thinking of all the horrible possibilities.

Viv couldn't help herself, so she butted in with that same booming voice again: "Buuuuyyyy Wiiiillllssss sooommmme coooonnnnddddoooommmms."

And with that comment, GiGi slapped the table with her right hand, snorted, and laughed out loud. She and Viv completely cracked up at Mary's expense. She tried to stop them: "This is not funny at all. You're both sick to laugh at such a thing...this is Wills we are talking about...and his life."

But the more she tried to get them to stop laughing, the more they cackled. And cackled. And cackled.

Finally, they settled down enough for Mary to speak again: "Listen, I'll talk to Philip about this and see what he thinks. I hate to say it, but maybe you're onto something. He hasn't spent a weekend at home in a few weeks, so he very well could be meeting a girl."

"Or porno...don't ever forget the porno, Mary," GiGi responded, as if Mary had forgotten a very important detail.

"I've got an idea," Viv interrupted. "Let's go through his room and see if we can find something...anything...that might give us a clue."

"Wills is too smart to leave any clues," answered Mary.

"Teenage boys are many things, but smart isn't one of them," chided GiGi. "Remind me again, *who* raised you?" GiGi motioned for Mary and Viv to follow her from the table as she made her way to Wills's room: "Teenage boys are naive and foolish. And the whole lot of them are so charged up with hormones that they can't think straight for a second. If they're not looking at porno, they're thinking about looking at it. Trust me on that, Mary."

The three spent the next hour combing Wills's room for clues, but they came up with nothing.

"I told you he was smart," said Mary proudly, as she put her hands on her hips and glanced around the room. "He may be naive and foolish"—catching her mother's eye, she persisted—"*and* he may even be thinking about porno or looking at porno, for all I know..."

Mary closed the bedroom door, leaving the room exactly as it had been found. As it shut, she went on, but this time with a booming voice, speaking very slowly: "Wiilllsss maaay eveeenn neeeddd sooommmme coonnnddoooommss beeccaaauussse heee isss haaavvviiinnngggg seeexxxx."

Then she stopped and looked at them both, letting the tone of her voice fall flat: "But he's smarter than the average teenage boy."

GiGi turned to Viv and said glibly: "He gets his smarts from me."

Mary was already down the stairs searching for her car keys, but she clearly heard the rest of her mother and Viv's conversation. Viv answered: "Yeah, he probably gets the porno from you too."

"Viv, hush your mouth! You are not too big for a big kick in the behind. What would my friends at church think if they heard you speaking like that?"

Viv rolled her eyes. "It was a joke, Mom. Just a joke."

Mary shouted out to them: "I'm leaving to pick up Tate and Miss Charity...lock up and let yourselves out once you finish the cat fight!"

On the drive to pick up her children, Mary's mind raced. All she could think about was talking to Philip.

Chapter 5

Philip and Mary talked late into the night, and they decided that Mary should begin calling around and speaking with other parents about what their children were doing on the weekends. She got on the task right away. After numerous conversations, she learned about Lemon Drop Parties, which were apparently soirees of dancing and mingling on Friday evenings that had become routine for juniors and seniors of the local high schools to attend. The social events were held at a different location each week, were for the most part totally unsupervised, and were described as harmless fun. More than one mom declared that the parties were better than having teenagers out cruising the streets looking for trouble, while two moms told Mary their daughters had mentioned seeing Wills at the parties. One said: "I was unsure about the parties until I heard Wills was going. He's always been such a good kid; he was like our seal of approval."

Mary called Philip, and they discussed what she had discovered. In short order, Wills would be staying home that weekend. They'd hog-tie him and lock him in his room if they had to, but Wills would not be going to a Lemon Drop Party until they had more information.

Meanwhile, Wills sat in third-period English class trying his best to focus on Mrs. Carter's instructions for the upcoming persuasive essay. But his mind refused to cooperate. He turned and looked across the room at Crew. The two had been best friends since middle school when Crew's family had moved from Atlanta after his father accepted the position of president at a Chattanooga bank. Wills still recalled the unforgettable day when Crew Cutless entered Ocoee Middle School. His blond hair and blue eyes caught the eye of every girl that day. While most eighth-grade boys were awkward and unsure, Crew had carried himself like royalty. He was a born leader; it was obvious, and Wills admired him for it. At lunchtime, Crew had chosen a seat next to Wills. The boys quickly learned that they both had a love for the game of football, and later that day, during an open PE class, they had thrown the ball to one another for the first time. The rest was history. The two had been pretty much inseparable ever since.

The bell rang, and Crew waited for Wills by the door.

"Hey, man, have I got some communiqué for you! Looks like a couple of senior girls from Baylor are coming down for the party this weekend!" Crew looked like he had been ripped out of the pages of an Abercrombie magazine; the students crowding the hallways seemed to part for him as he walked by. The teenage god gave them an obligatory nod as he continued to speak: "As you know, Baylor is full of exceedingly beautimus 'shes'...and we just so happen to be the most exceedingly beautimus 'hes' I know of...so. Go. Get. Your. Lemon. Drops!"

"Yeah, I think the fam has something planned for me this weekend, man," Wills answered while stopping at his locker to grab an algebra-two book.

Crew waited on his friend to shut his locker, put his arm around his neck, pulled him close, and whispered in his ear as they continued to walk down the busy hall. "Look, I know you're struggling with the whole Jesus and church thing, but you aren't breaking any rules. You haven't gone all the way with anybody...ever...probably haven't even come close, have you?" Wills didn't respond to the goading, so Crew went on: "And a little hit of weed is already legal in some states. You should try it sometime. Try it all, buddy, 'cause you only live once, right?" Pulling Wills's head down to his chest and messing up his hair with the ball of his fist, Crew clenched his teeth and assumed the character of a caveman as he announced: "We men, and we like Baylor wo-men!" Then he laughed and pushed Wills away from him, rushing off to his own class.

Friday night came quickly. Earlier in the week, Mary and Philip had held a meeting with Wills to inform him that they knew about the Lemon Drop Parties, were concerned about his change in behavior, and were forbidding him to go out over the weekend. When he came down the stairs, dressed and ready to go out, Mary and Philip were busy in the kitchen getting dinner together. Philip glanced up, immediately taking note of Wills's appearance. Tate was seated at the counter acting out scenes from the latest rerun of *I Love Lucy* for her parents, while Miss Charity sat in her high chair playing with the iPad.

Wills decided to take his parents head on. "I know you've forbidden me to go out this weekend, but I will be seventeen in a couple of weeks and think I am old enough to make my own decisions. So, I'll be going out this evening and won't be home until tomorrow around lunchtime. I'll be at Crew's house if you need to reach me."

Before Wills could round the corner toward the garage, Philip stepped in front of him and placed his hand firmly on his chest. "Son, I'm sorry, but you're not going anywhere. You may be turning seventeen, but your mother and I are still very much in charge."

What ensued from there was a blur. Talking turned to screaming. Screaming turned into pushing. And pushing ultimately left Philip flat on the floor. Tate cried hysterically, and Miss Charity, not understanding the mammoth ruckus and feeling quite distressed, beat her head and hands on the kitchen table multiple times. At some point during the upheaval, her high chair pushed away from the table. When her head came crashing down a final time, it found a corner, and blood spilled everywhere. Wills was gone, and Philip, Mary, and Tate were on the way to the hospital to get stitches for "Miss."

Poppy's message picked up after the fourth ring: "Leave a message, and I'll get right back to you. God bless, and have a great day!"

"Hey, Dad, it's me. Everything is OK, so don't panic. I need you to meet us at SkyRidge to pick up Tate. It looks like Miss Charity is gonna need some stitches tonight. Call me back."

Within minutes, GiGi and Poppy found Philip, Mary, Tate, and Charity at the hospital. A nurse had thoroughly cleaned Miss Charity's wound and left a large piece of gauze taped to her forehead to protect it while they waited on the doctor to come stitch her up. She had cried so fiercely that she was now sound asleep, unaware of what was going on around her...hopefully dreaming of something sweet. Mary filled her parents in on as many details as she could recall. Tate sat in a chair next to Philip, holding his hand, pretending not to listen.

GiGi, after hearing the evening's commotion recounted, leaned down and elbowed Philip on his arm. "Did Mary tell you my theory about Wills?"

"She did," Philip answered while rubbing his face with his free hand. He looked toward Mary, who was seated in a chair cradling Miss Charity in her arms, leaving thousands of tiny kisses on top of the little girl's head.

Poppy, Mary's father, overheard GiGi's question to Philip and quickly stepped in: "Let's get Tate and scoot out of here. There'll be plenty of time to talk about all of this tomorrow." Bending down on one knee in front of Tate, he smiled. "Wouldn't it be great fun if we had a campout in GiGi and Poppy's great room tonight? We'll pull out the sofa bed and stay up all night watching *I Love Lucy* reruns."

GiGi chimed in: "I'll make us some hot chocolate with marshmallows. What a fantastic idea, Pops!"

Philip pulled Tate's hand up to his mouth. He turned it so that he could kiss it, just as Prince Charming would kiss the hand of a princess. "Go and try to have some fun. We'll probably be here awhile longer, and you'll never get Poppy to agree to watch *I Love Lucy* again."

"But I don't want to leave. I'm scared something bad is gonna happen to Wills, and I think I need to be here with y'all," she answered.

Mary felt a couple of warm tears run down her face. "Wills is going to be just fine, because the Lord is protecting him. Teenagers act sort of weird sometimes, sweetheart; we just need to pray for him."

"But he pushed Daddy; I saw him do it, and that's not right," she insisted.

Mary thought for a moment about what she should say. "Have you ever gotten angry with Wills and given him a push?" she asked.

Tate just looked at her mom, her face giving away the answer.

"It's sort of the same thing," Mary explained. "Wills thought Daddy was being unfair to him, so he let his anger get the best of him and pushed Daddy. But look at him sitting there." Mary nodded toward Philip. "Does he look mad or hurt?"

Tate shook her head.

"Of course not, because he understands that Wills is just going through one of those strange teenage stages. Nobody's perfect, Tater Bug. Your brother just made a mistake; we'll sort it all out when he gets home. As for you, though, listen to your Poppy and scoot along. Go have some fun at GiGi and Pop's house tonight."

"Will you call Preacher Walker so he can pray for him?" asked Tate, now beginning to feel better about things.

"If I agree to call Preacher Walker and ask him to pray for Wills tonight, will you go have a campout with GiGi and Poppy?"

Tate looked around the room and thought about it. It was true that she would probably never get Poppy to agree to an *I Love Lucy* marathon again...and she did love hot chocolate with marshmallows: "Yes, I'll go if you'll promise to call my preacher so he can be praying."

It was nearly three o'clock in the morning when GiGi and Poppy finally nodded off to sleep. Their sofa bed was loaded with three bodies piled under blankets, their snoring competing with Lucy and Ricky Ricardo, who were still blaring through the surround-sound speakers. An opened bag of marshmallows sat on an end table, accompanying three very large mugs. Tummies were full, and hearts were at ease.

At Mary and Philip's house, the king-sized bed in the master bedroom was also loaded with three who were piled under blankets, snoring. Thankfully, Miss Charity had only needed some skin glue to close her wound instead of stitches. The bandage, pink and sparkly, would remain on her forehead for a few days. One of her arms was thrown over Philip's face, while a foot rested precariously on top of Mary's hip. Miss Charity sprawled across the entire bed, leaving Mary and Philip barely enough room. They each clung to their own sides, hoping to not be forced off the bed by their little sleeping beauty during the night. Trudy, the family's miniature black schnoodle, took her place at the end of the bed where it was safe. Having been accidentally shoved off the bed many times by a slumbering little girl, she knew better than to get too close to Miss Charity during the night. It was a sight to see.

When the cell phone rang, Philip sat straight up. He knew it wasn't going to be good news. Trudy, alerted by the sounds, was the only one in the bed who sat up with him.

Chapter 6

"Crew, is that you, son?"

Honestly, Philip did love Crew like a son. Sure, the kid was rough around the edges, always pushing the boundaries, but he'd been a loyal friend to Wills. In fact, Philip was one of the only people in the boy's life who could see through all the pomp and circumstance. While everyone else in town focused on his soap-opera-star looks, his charm, and his incredible athletic ability, Philip simply saw a boy who happened to be his son's very best friend.

Philip had given Crew a ride home after every football practice since the eighth grade when the boys played together the first time. He regularly inquired about Crew's test scores and report cards, and he often listened to Crew share his dreams for the future until the wee hours of the morning when he spent the night over at their house. The former high-school quarterback, now turned father, recalled only a handful of games when Crew's parents had come out to watch their son play ball; he couldn't recall ever having a real conversation with either his mom or his dad. Philip often wondered why the Cutlesses were distant and why they didn't make more time for their son, but he never discussed it with the fair-haired boy. He'd never even brought the subject up with Wills or with Mary. For Philip, in an odd sort of way,

Crew had offered an opportunity for him to expand his heart and to love another human being unconditionally, as he did his own children. Crew's faults were many and painfully obvious at times, but unconditional love never notices. Philip had looked past them all.

"Mr. Montgomery. I am so sorry." Crew could barely speak through the tears. His voice cracked with every word. Making no attempt to conceal his desperation, he cried in a hushed tone: "I need you to come get us right now!"

Philip somehow managed to find control. "Everything's gonna be OK, Crew; just tell me where you are." He didn't ask about Wills. Perhaps he was too afraid. The moment he saw Crew's cell-phone number appear on the screen of his own phone, he had determined not to ask any questions. His son was obviously in some kind of trouble; he'd get all the answers soon enough. First, though, he had to get to them.

As for Mary, she slept peacefully through it all. Philip clicked off the call and never turned back to check on her. Wearing a pair of flannel pajama pants, a short-sleeved white T-shirt, and some rag-wool socks, he drove out of the driveway and onto Ocoee Street. It would take him fifteen minutes to get to Mountain Brook, the place where Crew and Wills would be waiting for him. He knew it well, because GiGi and Poppy's home was in that particular neighborhood.

Thoughts raced through Philip's mind as he drove: *Why did Crew insist I pick them up next to the road? Away from houses? Away from the many families they know who live in the neighborhood? For that matter, why didn't they simply go wait at GiGi and Poppy's house? Wills knows where they hide their house key and could easily let himself in.*

It didn't make sense.

"Preacher." Philip woke him from a deep sleep. "I need to talk to you for a few minutes."

Preacher Walker knelt beside the worn recliner in his den after placing the phone back onto the receiver. Resting his elbows on the seat of the chair, he gently laid his face into the palms of his hands and began to weep. Seconds later, he was wailing out loud...there were moments when he could barely catch his breath. Jeannie, his bride of fifty-one years, heard the familiar sound coming from the softly lit corner room. As was her custom on evenings like this, she padded softly into the room. Kneeling beside her beloved husband, she wrapped her arms around his shoulders and pressed her head against his. The man with the gentle soul didn't utter a word. He literally cried out to Jesus on Wills's behalf.

Philip ran through every red light in town before finally arriving at the stone entrance. "OK, into the neighborhood...don't turn to go toward GiGi and Poppy's house; instead, follow the road on around to the left. Pass the white house on the right...and the boys should be beside some trees back off the road at the bottom of the hill..." Philip talked out loud to himself as he drove through Mountain Brook. "There's the white house...so, they must be..."

And then he saw Crew. The boy waved his arms and motioned for Philip to come. Philip pulled his vehicle next to the grass, slammed it into park, jumped out, and ran as fast as his legs would carry him.

Crew was in a panic and spoke in choppy, broken sentences: "He passed out...party down the street...the cops showed up...I grabbed Wills...ran out the back door...he tripped or something; I'm not sure what happened...then I dragged him down here."

By this time, Philip was leaning over his son, speaking to him: "Wills, can you hear me?" Wills didn't respond.

"Crew, you've gotta help me get Wills into the car. You have to calm down and work with me." Philip was still maintaining control. "I'm going to pull my car up as far as I can to this tree line. Just sit tight; we'll get him to the hospital, and everything will be OK."

Wills had made a few noises as Philip and Crew laid him in the backseat of the SUV. Philip thought that was a good sign.

As they drove toward the local hospital, Philip noticed Crew rocking back and forth. His hands trembled wildly, and his breathing came in quick spurts like the sound of a dog panting after a good squirrel chase. It worried Philip. "Crew, I think you may be going into shock. Let's slow that breathing down, all right? Take some deep breaths, in and out, or you're gonna pass out on me too. One of you has to stay with me, OK, son?"

Crew didn't answer. His whole body started to jerk as he rocked back and forth faster and harder. Philip spoke in an even tone: "Crew, buddy, I'm going to call your father and have him meet us at the hospital. I've got his cell number saved in my phone. No worries, just try to calm down and take long, smooth breaths. Everything is going to be fine."

Crew slammed his hands down against the dashboard, the booming sound causing Philip to nearly run off the road. He then followed the action with a scream. It was a guttural noise, unlike anything Philip had ever heard. "*Nooooo*, please God, *nooooo!*"

Philip kept driving. He didn't want to say anything else for fear of making things worse.

Crew, in full panic mode, looked down and found Philip's phone lying on the center console. In one quick motion, he rolled down the window and flung Philip's phone right out into the street. He continued to scream like a boy who'd gone mad: "*No, no, no!* Do you hear me? *Nooooo!*"

Crew grabbed fistfuls of his own hair and violently shook his head around while pitifully bawling the words "No, no, no" over and over and over again.

Philip finally answered the boy's cries. "OK, Crew, if you'll keep it together, I won't call your father. Obviously I can't call him now that you've tossed my phone out the window." Philip gave a sigh. "Just please stay with me!"

"God, I'm an idiot! I'm so sorry about your phone…I shouldn't have done that," he groaned. "I don't know why I did that, Mr. Montgomery. I just hate my life. I really, really hate my life." He finally leaned his head up against the passenger window and went to pieces, tears innumerable falling down his face.

"I'll replace that phone next week, Crew; it's really no big deal. Right now, just try your best to calm down for me."

They pulled into the emergency-room entrance and were met by a security guard. Within seconds, Wills was rushed back into a room to be examined. Philip watched the gurney roll out of sight and wished he could be by his son's side, but instead, he stood in the lobby holding Crew tightly in his arms. Crew was still shaking violently. His tears soaked Philip's T-shirt.

"I've gotcha, buddy," was all Philip could think to say, and he must have said the words fifteen or twenty times when Preacher Walker finally walked in.

"Go to Wills, and let me stay here with Crew," he encouraged. "I've called Mary, and she's droppin' Miss Charity off at her parents' house and then'll be on her way here shortly. There's nothin' quite like two visits to the hospital in a span of a few hours with two different kids, is there? I've been a pastor for a lotta years, but I think this is the first time I've ever seen it."

As Philip walked away, Preacher Walker put his arm around Crew and directed him over to an area that held a big, comfy couch. In the hour that followed, Preacher Walker learned all about Crew and his story. The boy had kept his family's secret long enough.

Chapter 7

When Philip reentered the waiting room, the ever-poised Mary was on his arm. Preacher Walker and Crew rose to greet them. Philip was eager to tell them the good news, so he didn't make them wait.

"He took a nasty knock to his head when he fell and has a pretty bad concussion. They've decided to keep him for a while for observation. They'll probably release him around dinnertime, but he won't be going back to school for a few days."

Mary broke in: "He has a horrible headache and is feeling nauseous and rattled, so I'm going to leave Philip with you guys and go back to sit with him. Maybe y'all could go grab some breakfast...the sun should be up any minute now, and it has been a very long night."

She released Philip and threw each of her arms around the necks of the pastor and the boy; she was facing them and pulled them close to her for a hug. "Thank you both for being here; we love you."

As she turned from them to walk away, Crew swiped a fresh set of tears from his face, while Preacher Walker chimed in: "You know, Philip, Crew and I were just discussing how hungry we are. It sure is awful nice of you to offer to take us out for a bite to eat." He turned to Crew, giving a quick wink: "Ain't that right, Crew?"

Philip answered for the teenager, who did look worn out and hungry: "I can take a hint...c'mon, guys, let's get out of here and find us some food."

The three found their way to a cozy, round table in a fast-food restaurant not too far from the hospital. The popular establishment was sure to feed many hungry guests in the coming hours; for now, though, it was empty and quiet, other than a few employees who busied themselves preparing food and cleaning windows. They filled their cups from the self-service drink station and made small talk about this and that. But Crew knew Philip would start asking questions at some point during breakfast. Mary wasn't kidding anyone; she had shoved them out of the hospital, together, so Philip could find out about last night. His stomach churned when he thought about it. At one point, he considered making an escape, perhaps retreating to the bathroom and then skipping out the back door when no one was looking. Instead, though, he chose to stick it out. He owed that much to Philip, Mary, and Wills.

"Crew, you were pretty shaken up last night, so I didn't ask any questions. But, son, no more fooling around; it's time. I need to know what happened."

The fair-haired boy, full of charisma, couldn't even look Philip in the face. All of his charm was gone. Useless to him. Again, tears began to stream down his face.

Preacher Walker spoke up: "Crew's got some good news, Philip." Placing his hand firmly on the boy's shoulder, he confidently nodded his head in Crew's direction while taking a big bite from his biscuit. His mouth was full when he continued, "You tell him the good news about what you did last night, Crew. Go ahead, tell him."

Philip's immediate response was to silently question what kind of good news could possibly have come from a night that had landed his son in a hospital bed with a major concussion. However, noting the calm assurance in the pastor's voice, he looked at the boy and decided to wait for a response. For the first time that morning, Crew looked up and met Philip's eyes.

"Look, Mr. Montgomery, I don't know why I'm here eating with you this morning. If I had anywhere else to go, I'd be there." He shifted his eyes toward the pastor, who was still chewing his biscuit, not willing to speak, not willing to give Crew a way out.

The most popular kid in town, the one who appeared to have the whole world by the tail, took a deep breath. "What Preacher Walker wants me to tell you is that I gave my heart to Jesus last night." Looking back to Philip, he said "I did, and I meant it with all of my heart. But I don't expect that to change anything. Wills could've died last night, and it would've been my fault. I don't think I'll ever forgive me, so I don't expect you to."

Philip's entire countenance changed. A load was lifted, making him feel as light as a feather; the heaviness that had been weighing on his shoulders, the heaviness he hadn't known had been there, disappeared. It began with a stab of pain that traveled from his heart, up through his throat, and came out of his mouth in the form of a gasp. At once, it felt like freedom and sheer elation.

"I have prayed for you for so long. God, you'll never know how I've prayed!" He noisily scooted his chair over as close as he could get to Crew and gave him a tremendous bear hug, not attempting to hide his overwhelming emotions. "Crew, there is no forgiveness needed, because I never held anything against you. You are like a son to me. It would be impossible for me not to love you."

Crew couldn't hold it in. He thought he'd cried out every tear in his body during the last few hours, but somehow his eyes found more. They poured, and with the release flowed the many years he had felt unloved and neglected, like he wasn't worthy of belonging.

Philip allowed him to cry for a few minutes, until he couldn't contain his own joy any longer. Without warning, he jumped up from his chair and flung his hands up into the air: "Wahoo! Hallelujah! Thank You, Jesus, for saving Crew!" Clapping his hands, he continued, his voice profound, nearly in song: "This is the day the Lord has made, and so I'm gonna rejoice and be glad in it!"

All the workers in the restaurant looked up and either giggled or shook their heads. It didn't matter to Philip. He kept shouting with his head thrown straight back and eyes now closed: "Thank You, Jesus! Oh, thank You, thank You, thank You, sweet Jesus!" Crew was stunned, but not embarrassed. A silly grin spread out across his face. When Philip finally sat back down, he gave Crew a big pat on the back. "God is so good. In the midst of all the turmoil, He was coming through to surprise us with a miracle!"

The entire time, the preacher had simply sat back and taken it all in. He knew Philip so well and had guessed what his reaction would be. To see it played out in front of him was beautiful for him to behold; it made the hard work of being a pastor worth it all. He kept smiling and eating his biscuit while Philip talked, talked, and talked some more.

Philip couldn't shut up. "You're like the story of the Prodigal Son who ran from God for such a long time...you never would go to church with us, and I couldn't understand why...I just knew I needed to love you and pray for you. And then today, you've come home...I'm just so thankful...Wills is going to be thrilled..."

Preacher Walker watched Crew closely as Philip testified about the goodness of God. The man with the gentle soul knew how difficult it was going to be for Crew to share his secret with Philip; he also knew how difficult all of it was going to be for Philip to bear.

This was an appointed time; the fiercely guarded secret would finally be shared today. The long-carried burden lifted. It was now evident to the elder man how each event that had occurred over the last several days, and even the last several hours, had been meticulously planned out and executed by the very hand of God. It had all been used to lead them to this place and time.

Yes, he and Philip had cried out in prayer for Wills over the past weeks, but soon Philip would understand what the old man already knew. The heaviness they had been feeling in their hearts was for Crew, not Wills. And the prayers they had been praying for Wills were actually set into action for the benefit of Crew.

In the next few minutes, whenever Philip stopped talking long enough to take a breath, another piece of God's puzzle would find its place in the whole scheme of their lives. Lessons would be learned, lives would be forever changed, and each would grow ever closer to their Creator. The man with the gentle soul reveled in the ways of God.

Chapter 8

"It's been two weeks, Mary. We have to eventually address this. You know you can't go on avoiding the subject forever."

Miss Charity, at five years of age, was not yet potty trained, so Mary knelt on the floor changing her diaper and getting her dressed for the day. She continued to focus on her little angel girl, ignoring Philip, who was bent on talking to her about Crew's family situation. Sensing the tension between her parents, the little one flashed her bright eyes up at her daddy, giving him a big smile. Her best effort at cuteness, however, did not deter him from the task at hand.

"Please think about Crew sleeping in that basement, night after night, locked off from his parents. Mary, we have to offer our home to him."

She gathered Miss Charity into her arms, stood with her back to Philip, and made her way to the kitchen for breakfast. Philip read her intent loud and clear.

GiGi and Poppy were already seated at the table, each on either side of Tate, when Mary entered the room. They were feasting on a box of Daylite Bakery doughnuts while watching a gripping episode of *Scooby Doo*. Mary felt feisty and didn't hesitate to show it.

"Really? Doughnuts? 'Miss Miss' will be bouncing off the walls within minutes of eating one of those, and you know it."

"Who says she'll eat just one?" Poppy asked while popping the last bite of a chocolate-covered piece of heaven into his mouth.

Miss Charity took one look at the doughnuts and hastily squirmed right out of her momma's arms.

"Come to your GiGi, honey. I brought you doughnuts 'cause I love ya!" Then, shooting a sideways glance to Mary, GiGi said: "A little sugar never hurt anybody; we'll just bounce off the walls together!"

"Well, she's all yours for the next couple of hours, so you'll have plenty of time to enjoy your bouncing! But only one doughnut, all right?" Mary hopped up and down pretending to be a bouncing bunny as she kissed each one on the top of the head. First GiGi, then Tate, next Poppy...but when Mary reached Miss Charity, the last one to receive the silly hopping kiss, the little girl looked straight up so that Mary's kiss would land on her already sugar-covered lips. "Stinker!" Mary proclaimed, to which Miss Charity wrinkled her nose, smiled, and continued to chew her doughnut.

Philip tied his tie, slipped on his shoes, and made a stop by the kitchen to find Mary had already gone. "Thanks for coming over to stay with the kids this morning so Mary could pick up Wills's schoolwork. The doc says he might be able to return to school next week. I think the headaches are finally improving."

After filling a cup with coffee, he took a seat across from Tate and helped himself to a sugary treat. Miss Charity, sitting in her chair at the end of the table, tossed the remains of a doughnut at her daddy with a giggle. "Throwing food now, are we, Miss?" In turn, he picked it up and threw it right back at her. Her giggling turned into full-blown laughter with snorts and all. He found a doughnut covered with colorful sprinkles to slide across the table like a hockey puck. It slowed down to a stop in front of the little girl's hands, who scooped it up with lightning speed. "Well, that's one way to teach her not to throw food." Philip was pleased with himself.

Mimicking Philip's statement, GiGi threw her two cents in with a slightly mocking tone: "Teaching her now, are we, Dad? You'll be lucky if Mary doesn't shoot you for giving her that extra doughnut."

"She's not happy with me right now anyway, so what's an extra doughnut going to hurt?"

GiGi and Poppy knew better than to respond with Tate sitting there, so they said nothing. He went upstairs to check on Wills, who, according to the doctor's orders, had to stay in a dark room as much as possible in order to heal. Then he thanked his in-laws again for helping out with the kids and left for work.

Just a few houses down the street, Crew's morning held the same routine as it had for as many years as he could remember. His alarm woke him at 5:45 a.m. He showered, dressed, made himself a piece of toast, and went out the basement door without seeing his mother. The door to the upstairs, to the area where his mom always lived and where his dad rarely lived, was locked. He didn't need to check it. It had been locked since the day they moved in. If he wanted to see his momma, he had to knock loudly and request entrance. Sometimes she allowed it, but on most days she didn't. Lately, he hadn't knocked.

Crew had his own entrance to the basement from the outside, had been given an unlimited credit card to take care of all of his needs, as well as a cell phone, and on his sixteenth birthday, his father had bought him a car for transportation. Things had been trickier before he could drive, so on the first day of ownership, he gave his car a befitting name: "Liberty." He admitted to himself on many occasions what a wonder it was that he had successfully held the family secret for such a long time. Was he that good an actor, or did people simply not care enough to notice the oddities in his life? Thoughts began to rush through his mind as he drove to school: *I told them everything, but it hasn't changed anything. Why haven't they reached out to help me more? Sure, they call to check on me every day, telling me they are working things out, but if I have to live like this much longer, I'm going to be as batty as Momma.*

The teenager had allowed himself to dream that Preacher Walker and Philip would step in to save him from the abyss of loneliness, fear, and rejection. His heart began to pound hard as his thoughts grew more intense.

Maybe this Jesus thing isn't real. Yeah, I was probably a fool to fall for it. A loving God would never let a kid live the life I've lived. And He wouldn't let a woman go crazy either. They blame me that Wills is still having those headaches. And they probably hate me for dragging him to the Lemon Drop Parties. I was an idiot for thinking things could get better.

Despair crept into the car, while anguish threatened to overwhelm him. As he choked back tears, his hands began to tremble. Another panic attack was coming. Within minutes, his mind wouldn't allow him to think clearly. He had an urge to push the gas pedal down to the floor and fly off the road into a deep ditch, but at the same time, he had an urge to drive to the hospital to beg for help. His heart raced wildly, like it might pop out of his chest. Then his mind cleared to a single thought: *Marijuana is hidden under the passenger's seat.* It was as if the words had been whispered into his ear. He hadn't used since the night of the party, since the night he became a "Christian." What good had it done him?

Crew pulled off into a residential neighborhood near the school and parked his car in the driveway of an empty home that had been for sale for quite some time. Knowing it would be unlikely for a realtor to show a house so early in the morning, he'd frequented this particular home several times without being noticed. After smoking for a few minutes, the fair-haired boy who had recently given his heart to an unseen God pulled into the school parking lot feeling fearless, relaxed, and ready to take his place as the most popular kid in school.

Angels had been diligently at work all around Crew, but he couldn't see them or hear them. Every night, when he thought he was coming home to an empty basement to eat yet another dinner alone, they were waiting for him. They sat with him as he ate and remained with him while he did his homework. At night, while he lay in his bed fighting fear, searching aimlessly for sleep, they stood watch over him, singing songs of hope to him. And it was also the angels who were prompting the minds of Preacher Walker and Philip throughout the day, encouraging them to find a solution for Crew and urging them to call and check on him when he was at his lowest.

On the other side, however, were the dark ones who were equally intent on bringing hopelessness to Crew. He had unknowingly entertained them for such a large part of his life that falling into their trap of despair came too easy. Both the angels of light and the angels of darkness were present in the parking lot of Bradley High School when Crew pulled in and parked Liberty. Crew had no idea how much work had gone into this moment. He didn't know how pivotal his salvation had been for the thousands he was to touch with his life. The angels, in one accord, sang, "Hang on to Jesus," while the dark ones looked on with resolve and contempt.

"Crew! Hey, buddy! I need to talk to you for a few minutes!" Crew heard the sound and recognized the voice. He caught a glimpse of the old pastor waving his arms as he walked from the front of the school toward Crew. "I decided to do my prayer walk early this morning so I could see you before school! Wait up!" Preacher Walker picked up his pace.

Crew forced the slight glimmer of hope from his mind and chose despair instead. "I'm late for a meeting. I'll catch you another time!" Grabbing his backpack, he raced into the school, never looking back.

Over the past two weeks, the pastor and his wife had been preparing a bedroom for Crew in their own home. It was to be a place of refuge. He'd come early to the school to surprise Crew with the news, but the freshly saved teenage boy wouldn't find out about it anytime soon. He was putting Jesus and His followers behind him.

Chapter 9

Mary returned home with Wills's schoolwork and found GiGi and Poppy seated in the great room keeping up with the latest ramblings on the Fox News channel. She quickly noticed how they'd taken the time to clean the clutter in her house, and she felt her heart swell out of love for them. She had felt so worn out lately from all the stress surrounding Wills that she barely found the energy to keep up with the laundry, much less the rest of the house. Her parents had ministered to her today without realizing it.

GiGi turned around in her seat, gave Mary a darted point of her finger, and motioned for her to quietly have a look upstairs. In response, Mary removed her shoes, tiptoed up the stairs and down the hall, and stopped just in front of Wills's room.

"And then the fairy princess climbed the tree to save the little kitty cat. She was afraid to go up so high, but she kept climbing up higher and higher and higher..."

Mary crept into the room and interrupted Tate's story.

"So, I leave the house for a little while and return to find I am not even needed around here. Look at you, Miss Charity and Tate, taking such good care of your big brother! You guys sure do look mighty comfy piled up in the bed."

Tate was laying her head on Wills's right shoulder, while Miss Charity had tucked herself underneath his left arm. The little munchkin had placed her prized princess crown on Wills's head; he gave his mom a smirky smile, letting her know he didn't mind it at all. Mary took a few steps and then lay down across the foot of the bed. "Go ahead, Tate; I can't wait to hear the end of your story!"

Her middle child was happy to continue: "So, the princess climbed all the way to the top, carefully rescued the frightened kitten, and brought her down to the little boy who was waiting below. The princess faced her fears that day and saved the kitten from danger, making the entire village love her even more. From that day forward, she was known as a fearless hero! The end."

Miss Charity did her sign for "more," moving her hands back and forth quickly as the ends of her fingers touched in front of her.

"You want more, do you?" Mary asked her. The little girl's eyes grew wider as she anticipated what might come next. "Tate, how about we give this little girl a visit from the tickle monster instead?"

Mary grabbed Miss Charity's little feet and started tickling them while Tate tickled underneath her chin. Wills, caught in the middle, pretended to be a knight coming to save the princess from the terrible Tickle Monsters. Miss Charity relished every second. For her, this was the ultimate life!

At the same time that the infamous Tickle Monster was visiting Miss Charity, Preacher Walker was walking into Philip's office to discuss Crew's strange behavior at the school.

"Philip, I'm sure sorry to bother you at work. You know I'd never come by and interrupt unless it was terribly important."

"Are you kidding? You are always welcome here! Come in and take a seat."

The pastor gave Philip the whole story, and they both sat for a few minutes in silence as they contemplated what had happened. Philip tapped his fingers on his desk while thinking out loud: "Preacher, maybe it was because he was at school...around his peers. You know teenagers get funny about that kind of thing. I've been talking to him every day, and he seems to be hanging in there very strong."

"Well, I've been thinking the same thing. He always seems real happy to hear from me. Maybe I shoulda told him about the room Jeannie and I've been gettin' ready for him, but I wanted to make it a silly surprise. He seemed real hurt at me today."

The two finally agreed they would send a text to Crew's cell phone, inviting him to meet them at the Rebel restaurant after school at 2:45 p.m.

"It would be better for us to meet with him and to know what's going on than to sit around and guess about it," Philip remarked while punching in the text message.

Preacher Walker started walking toward the door. "See you this afternoon for a Lotta Burger and tater tots; what do you say?"

"A Lotta Burger it is! And how 'bout a cherry Coke to wash it all down?" Philip asked.

"You do know the language of friendship, don't ya?" And with that, the man with the gentle soul closed the door and left.

At 2:35 p.m., Preacher Walker and Philip were in a booth by the window waiting on Crew. By 3:00 p.m., they realized he wasn't coming.

Crew had received the text during fourth-period study hall but didn't answer it. He used the remaining time in study hall to decide how he would deny everything he ever told the pastor and Philip, should it become necessary. He was going back to the life he knew. It wasn't a perfect life, but it kept him from having to depend on other people.

At 2:30 p.m., when the school bell rang to signal the end of the day, Crew was busy inviting everyone to the next Lemon Drop Party. He was outside in the parking lot, surrounded by a small throng of his schoolmates, who were unaware he was keeping such a close eye on the highway running in front of the school. He thought he saw Preacher Walker's old baby-blue Volkswagen bug trudging toward the Rebel just before he announced: "This Friday night, the party is at my house. Everybody plan to stay the night!"

As Crew pulled away from the school, he felt pleased with himself and in control again. A thought of Wills entered his mind, but he pushed it out. Yeah, they'd been friends for a very long time, but all good things must end at some point. Wills had been beating him over the head with the Jesus stick long enough. He'd given it a try, but it wasn't for him. And all those times Wills had come to "chaperone" the Lemon Drop Parties, well, that was over as well.

When Crew sat down to eat his takeout dinner later that evening, as usual, he thought he was all alone. But he wasn't. In the place of the unseen angels were the dark ones. Three of them had been at the table, making small talk, waiting for him to arrive. They had gathered to celebrate Crew. He was the one, the special one, who had been called by their leader to be a stumbling block for thousands. They waited for him to pour a soda and sit at the table before they began their worship of him. Theirs was a haunting chant, eerily familiar to Crew's spirit. Although he couldn't hear the rich bass tones audibly, the words rang down deep in his soul, filling him with a renewed energy, strength, and fervor.

"Crew is a god! Worthy of praise! High and mighty is he!"

The sound was very much like an old gospel spiritual; it grew with intensity as they sang.

"Crew is a god! Worthy of praise! High and mighty is he!"

Over and over again they chanted the song, until they were up from their seats and bowing at Crew's feet with unseen hands raised to him.

"Crew is a god! Worthy of praise! High and mighty is he!"

Without knowing why, Crew began to hum a tune as he ate. It was a tune he couldn't place or recall hearing before. He liked it very much. So there he sat, eating his last bites of food while three demons bowed all around him chanting to the tune he hummed. It was otherworldly. Demonic. But chillingly beautiful.

He ate the last bite of food, rolled the paper products into a ball, and placed them in the sack. He almost stood to throw it all away in the nearby trash can but felt an urge to stay seated and speak his thoughts out loud: "Why did I ever think I needed Jesus?"

With one accord, the demons rose and left the room. Their work was done.

Chapter 10

"I'm telling you, Mare-Bear, the *'Po-Po'* are gonna *blow* this thang up *mondo*." Mary's sister, Viv, often used rhymes, trying to be hip and kitschy, when she was wound up. "Listen, I've gotta get to work before I'm late." She kissed her sister on the cheek before exiting. "Talk to Philip about this mess, and see what he can do!"

Mary, still in her pajamas, returned to her favorite chair to continue her Bible study. She folded her legs up under her and thought about the morning she had already had with her sister.

It began when Mary was sitting reading her Bible next to the window, as she did every morning at this time. She'd heard a peck on the window and immediately thought of the cardinal who often pecked at his reflection in the early-morning hours. She turned her head to look toward the sound of the *peck...peck...peck*. Instead of a red bird, however, she found her sister's face peering in at her, nose smashed up on the glass. She'd nearly had a heart attack but somehow managed to keep from screaming.

"What are you doing, scaring me like that?" Mary opened the door to let Viv come running in.

Viv darted right past Mary and into the hall bathroom, leaving a small crack open in the door so she could talk. She tried to hold back laughter but didn't manage it very well. "If you could have seen your face...*gah!* I wish I'd thought to record it so I could've had a viral video...I nearly peed my pants!"

Mary stood outside the bathroom door waiting on her sister to stop making light of a situation that still had her heart thumping. "Do you want a cup of coffee?"

"Are you on the crazy bus this morning? I'm getting ready to spend the day with a bunch of elementary-school kids; of course I want a cup of coffee! Stop pouting around and get to pouring!"

Although no one could see her, Mary didn't hide the roll of her eyes. It was very early. Everyone except for Trudy the dog was still sleeping, so she quietly poured the coffee and waited in the front den for Viv to join her.

"Lord, I did sprinkle some tinkle when I scared you. I'll probably be smelling like pee all day long. If a kiddo asks, I'll just sniff right along with them and act like I'm looking for where the smell is coming from. You know kids don't miss a thang...they'll smell it and start looking for the culprit!" Viv, who worked as a roaming physical therapist making regular visits to all the elementary schools in the county, took her coffee and found a seat in the cozy room.

Mary couldn't help but giggle. Her sister was a nut. "OK, Viv, I know if you got up this early, you have something important to talk to me about. I've already investigated your left hand for a sparkly diamond...so, if an engagement isn't the news of the day...what is?"

"Way to pour salt all over the old spinster lady's wounded heart; that man is slower than a herd of turtles moving through spilt molasses. If I wasn't so crazy about him, and if he wasn't such a high-powered lawyer with a load of cash-ola, I'd have to dump him and move on to the next lucky guy!"

"He'll come through. I have a good feeling about this one," Mary answered while taking a sip of coffee.

"I've got earth-shattering news, and here you are getting me off the subject. But before we get into it, how's Wills?"

"The doctor says he can return to school on Monday. He's followed all the rules...hasn't watched TV, played video games, or used his cell phone to text in two full weeks. That's a huge feat for a teenager."

"Are we still on for his birthday party tomorrow?"

"Yes, of course. I can't believe he's turning seventeen. I wanted to make it a big celebration, but after all he's been through, I think just having family around will be perfect."

"Well, I'll pick up the cake from the Village Bake Shop this afternoon, along with five dozen thumbprint cookies."

"Five dozen thumbprint cookies? We only need three dozen."

"And three dozen you will receive. The other two dozen are for me!"

Mary shook her head and grinned, thinking of all the years they had eaten their own birthday cakes and thumbprint cookies from that same little bakery in the old Village Mall. When Mary was growing up, she spent many summers working at Margaret's Dress Shop and Miller's Department Store. They were both gone now. All that was left of the old mall and those memories was the bakery.

"Back to the subject, Viv."

"Yes, back to the subject: Lemon Drop Parties." Viv was more than eager to deliver the juicy gossip.

"Oh no, I think I'd rather talk about thumbprint cookies and men who are afraid to pop the question. I thought Lemon Drop Parties were a thing of the past."

"Apparently not. Crew has ditched Jesus and is having another party in his basement. But that's not the worst part of it..."

Mary couldn't help herself; she butted in: "Ever since your dreamboat attorney found out about what was happening at those parties...just thinking about it makes me want to strangle that boy.

Exchanging lemon drops for indiscriminate sexual favors drawn out of a box is so vile and immoral."

"Well, listen." Viv regained control of the conversation. "The party is being raided. The cops took those kids they caught from that last party two weeks ago and made a deal that they wouldn't press any charges as long as those kids agreed to cooperate. In this case, cooperation means they have to rat out Crew's parties. At least one of them has followed through. The next party is tonight."

"After all the danger he subjected Wills to." Mary was so angry she could barely speak. "And dragging my son to those trashy parties..."

Viv interrupted: "Mary, what if Crew's story is true? What if his mother is suffering from a serious mental illness, and what if his father rarely comes home anymore? If he's really living in that basement, all alone night after night, I can almost see why he'd turn to drugs and wild parties. He's still a kid."

"Philip has been playing that same guilt trip on me. You're wasting your time. I'm a mother, and my main job is to protect my own children, not somebody else's depraved kid. Whatever is going on at those parties is so bad that the guilt nearly turned Wills away from all of us. He says he wasn't participating in that Lemon Drop madness, but who knows, right? He's a teenage boy surrounded by half-naked teenage girls...anything can happen in a situation like that."

"I believe Wills was going to those parties to look out for his friends. I think he's telling the truth about that. But I better *never* see him with a box of lemon drops...'cause if I do, the jig is up...know what I mean?" Viv tried to lighten things up by inserting humor into the conversation. It didn't work.

"Viv, when those two boys ran out of that house in the middle of the night, anything could've happened. Crew had been smoking pot and drinking alcohol, so he wasn't thinking straight. And Wills is so gullible and naive. We're fortunate he fell and hit his head, because it could've been much worse. What if Wills had gotten into a car with Crew or someone else who had been drunk or high?"

"But he didn't. And he's going back to school and back to some sort of normalcy on Monday. Your son loves Crew Cutless like a brother. I don't know what he'll do if something happens to him. A scandal like this could take away that boy's chances of a college scholarship. I'm sure Crew has never even thought about that."

After Viv left, Mary sat with her Bible and opened her Bible-study book up to the next passage of scripture:

2 Corinthians 2:5–8

But if anyone has caused harm, he has not so much harmed me as he has—and I don't think I'm exaggerating here—harmed all of you. *In my view*, the majority of you have punished him well enough. So instead of continuing to ostracize him, I encourage you to offer him *the grace of* forgiveness and the comfort *of your acceptance.* Otherwise, *if he finds no welcome back to the community,* I'm afraid he will be overwhelmed with extreme sorrow and lose all hope. So I urge you to demonstrate your love for him once again.

Mary slammed her Bible-study book shut. Typically she would've bowed and prayed in her chair, but not today. Trudy followed her into the kitchen. She washed out her coffee cup, reached underneath the sink to get a dog treat, and heard a still, small voice:

What if Crew needs you to be his momma?

Mary couldn't see the messenger standing next to her, but she heard his question loud and clear in her heart. She gave the dog a treat and then went to Miss Charity's room. Before opening the door, she could hear the little girl's snore. Without making a sound, she turned the handle and sat in the floor next to the toddler bed. Tears ran down her cheeks.

"Lord, I'm going to remind You of something. You've given me a lot to bear with Miss Charity. Every day, I wonder how much longer she'll live until her heart acts up again. And if that's not enough, You haven't given her the ability to communicate. How in the world can I meet all of her needs when I don't even know what her needs are? And then there's her sensory issues. Taking her out in public is getting more and more difficult. She melts down and wants to be carried, to hide her face in my neck, but she is getting heavy for me to carry. Wills and Tate are so amazing. I know they would love to have more one-on-one time with me, but they always have to share with this little munchkin. Trying to be everything to everyone is wearing me out. I barely have an ounce of energy to give to my husband, my parents, my sister and friends. Hear me loud and clear on this: I will *not* take on Crew Cutless and all of his issues. I will *not* bring a pot-smoking, alcohol-drinking, sex-addicted teenage boy into my home, and I will certainly *not* be his mother. I can't do it, Father. I just can't do it."

Mary's head was bowed in her hands. Tears were flowing so fast. Trying to wipe them away while she prayed, Mary was too focused to notice the little girl get out of her bed. As a result, she was surprised when she felt little arms wrap around her neck from behind. But Mary didn't turn to look at Miss Charity; instead, she stayed in the moment and allowed her little girl to bring much-needed comfort to her.

The unseen angel who had been in the kitchen earlier with Mary was now kneeling beside her. His shoulder touched hers. He looked at Miss Charity, who, unlike her momma, could see and hear him clearly: "That's right, sweet one; just keep loving on your momma."

In response, the little one with the extra chromosome reached one of her hands over and placed it on top of the angel's head. His hair was long and silky. Black as coal. Soft as a bunny. He reached up, took her hand from his head, and kissed it. She grinned and then brought her arm back around her mother's neck and squeezed her tight. Mary could've sworn she heard Miss Charity say, "Love you," but she quickly reminded herself that God had not given her little girl the gift of words.

Her shoulders began to shake as her tears turned into sobs. The angel continued to kneel in wonder at what was playing out before him. He too prayed: "Blessed Father, You are always right." Then he chuckled: "It is the weak who lead the strong."

Chapter 11

Mary and Philip were unaware their son had found out about Crew's next Lemon Drop Party. It was true that Wills hadn't been texting since the concussion, but today was different. His headaches were all but gone, and he felt better than he'd felt in days. When Crew didn't answer his text, Wills knew something wasn't right. He'd spent the entire morning getting to the bottom of the situation by texting several different friends. He checked the time on his cell phone when realization hit him: he had twelve hours to stop his best friend from having the party.

"Hey, sport!" Philip came in and sat on the end of his son's bed before leaving for work. "Can you believe this is your last day of playing hooky from school? It's back to the old grind early Monday morning!" Philip gave Wills a few loud pats on his legs as he spoke.

Playing along with his dad's humor, Wills answered, "Yeah, I guess I've used a bump on the head as an excuse long enough."

"Hey, by the way, have you heard from Crew the last couple of days?" Philip awkwardly changed the subject.

"No, but I'm not surprised. He's busy, and I've been a real bore lately."

Philip patted the tall teenager's very long legs one more time. Not wanting to give him any reason for alarm, he continued: "You're probably right. He's busy."

"And I've been boring."

Philip smiled. "Yep, I guess you have been boring. But who knows, maybe that knock to the head has knocked some irresistibility into you. Look out, ladies; my boy is back in business come Monday morning!"

Wills had such a good relationship with his dad, who had completely forgiven him for the way he'd treated his family before that last party...before the concussion. As he showered and got dressed for the day, he wondered if he should have told his dad about the Lemon Drop Party at Crew's house that night. But fear had taken over. How could he ever fully explain what went on at those parties? Sure, his dad knew about the weed, the beer, and the girls...but in reality, he didn't know the half of it.

Wills still couldn't get the things he saw and experienced at those parties out of his mind. The more he tried to forget, the more he seemed to remember. He talked himself into believing that the concussion served as a sort of punishment for his sins...God's way of getting his attention. He'd rationalized that he had paid for his sins, so there was no need for him to tell his parents or anyone else about what he'd done. It was better, he decided, for his parents to believe he'd only gone to those parties as a pseudochaperone, the good Christian boy trying to keep Crew and his other friends out of trouble.

That had been his intention...but then he'd fallen. Not every time, but some of the time. Sure, he had warned his friends every day how they were all going against God. How they might all go to hell for it. He had worn his conviction like a banner for everyone to see. His friends had even started calling him "Preacher Boy," which he resented. It made him feel even more like a hypocrite, since he was really no better than them. His friends knew it, and he knew it too. Maybe he hadn't gone as deep into sin as some of the others had, but he'd gone deep enough. Wills knew God didn't rate the severity of sin...to God, sin is simply sin.

This time, though, things would be different. This time he wouldn't go in falsely thinking he was strong enough to chaperone teenage debauchery; this time he was going to stop the madness altogether before he had the chance to fall again. Selfishly, he needed those parties to stop for his own sake most of all. Because if they continued, deep down he knew he would go back. Temptation was already wooing him, beckoning him to drink from the fountain of lust once again.

Wills wandered down the steps with his school books under his arm and found his way to the kitchen table. Tate was already seated, munching on an apple while working on her homeschool

English lesson. She looked up and was thrilled to see her brother finally coming out of his room:

"Hey, Wills! Whatcha doin'?" Her smile beamed, lighting up the entire room.

"Well, I thought I'd do my schoolwork this morning with one of my favorite people." He looked around the room, pretending to be searching for someone. "So, where is Miss Charity, anyway?"

Wills quickly laid his books on the table before grabbing a Pop-Tart from the pantry, waiting on Tate's return. "Wills Montgomery! You are so mean!"

Her big brother pushed his chair as close as he could get it to Tate, took a seat, and gave her his best puppy-dog eyes: "Can you take a joke and make some room for me at this humble kitchen table?"

"Yeah, I think I can make room for you! But no, I can't take your jokes...so cool it!" Tate giggled. She was so happy to have Wills up and about again.

Mary came into the kitchen with Miss Charity hanging on her hip.

"Well, would you look who's decided to come back to the land of the living, Miss Miss? Wonders never cease!"

Wills, with a mouth full of food, gave his mom a widemouthed, goofy grin, displaying chewed-up Pop-Tart.

Mary pursed her lips with sarcasm. "And oh, joy! He's even found some of his old preconcussion spunk!"

She walked over to him, placed her hand over his wide grin, effectively hiding the half-chewed Pop-Tart, and then planted a kiss on top of his head. Miss Charity, leaning over from Mary's hip, gave him a kiss of her own...just like her momma, she kissed him right on top of his head.

They all sat at the table together eating breakfast, working on schoolwork, discussing Wills's recovery, and planning Wills's birthday celebration. Sunshine poured through the windows, bringing with it warmth and a good mood for all.

By six o'clock, Philip lumbered into the home, finding Wills and Tate piled up on the couch battling one another in a game on their cell phones, while Mary worked through a preschool game on the iPad with Miss Charity in a nearby chair. Philip and Mary had not spoken to one another very much since their last confrontation about Crew, and Tate was catching on. Wills, though, who had spent the last two weeks in his room, hadn't a clue about his parents' disagreement.

"Hey, Daddy! Are you and Momma going on a date tonight? Wills is feeling much better and can babysit us!" Tate hoped to plant an idea that would stick in her father's head.

Before Philip could speak, Wills answered: "That sounds like a great idea! Mom deserves a night out, since all she's been doing lately is taking care of me."

Mary pretended to be too engrossed in the game to hear.

Philip pounced on the opportunity to force his wife's hand. If he could get her out alone, he figured she'd have to listen to his opinion about what they should do to help Crew.

"That sounds like a fantastic idea! I'm going to go change my clothes right now and get ready to take my bride out to dinner and a movie!"

He knew Mary had heard every word, even though her eyes never left the iPad.

Philip did a silly skip through the great room, never looking at Mary, but making his point loud and clear: "Yippee! A date night with the most beautiful gal in town!" He jumped up and clicked his heels before entering the master bedroom.

Mary turned to look at Wills and Tate, hoping to find an escape. Tate was grinning from ear to ear, proud of her accomplishment, while Wills appeared a bit bewildered. "I think that man is excited about date night, Mom!"

Turning back around toward the iPad, Mary softly whispered in Miss Charity's ear: "Looks like Momma's been trapped. I'm sorry, little bit, but you're on your own with this iPad for the rest of the night."

When she entered the master bath, Philip was singing a familiar song by Cool and the Gang: "Cel-e-brate good times, c'mon...doo, doo, doo, dah, doo, dah, dah, doo...cel-e-brate good times, c'mon..."

Mary couldn't help but give a slight chuckle at the sight of her husband dancing around in his boxer shorts, white undershirt, and black dress socks that were pulled up clear to his bony knees. He danced around like a bad act on *Soul Train* while singing completely out of tune. Ignoring her chuckle, he kept singing as Mary powdered her nose, applied lip gloss, and left the room.

"I'll meet you in the car!" she shouted, marching out of the bathroom and through the master bedroom.

Philip, making an intentional attempt to warm his wife's heart, turned his volume up much louder, nearly screaming the words: "Cel-e-brate good times, c'mon!"

Mary felt herself start to snicker but then remembered how aggravated she was, and needed to remain, at her husband. She said quick good-byes to her kiddos and scooted out the door to wait for her *Soul Train* husband in the car. All Wills could say was "Good luck with the Chief tonight," as he nodded his head toward the sound still blaring from the master-bath area. Mary knew her son had no idea how prophetic his words were. Philip was pulling out all the stops tonight: dinner, a movie, and a sense of humor. She would have trouble remaining strong for very long. She thought about her husband and his skinny, white legs dancing around the bathroom in boxer shorts and giggled.

"Oh, Mary, get it together. He's already breaking you down."

With Mary and Philip gone, Wills frantically began to plot how he would stop Crew from having his party. It was 6:30 p.m., half an hour until party time. Crew still hadn't responded to any of his texts.

Chapter 12

Every human being is divinely created for a purpose, meaning each detail of life, the highs and the lows, the twists and turns, are all measured out carefully for an eternal intent. If one could go back in time, to the beginning of time, perhaps the Montgomery family and the Cutless family were created so their paths would find a crashing intersection at this point in history.

What if God crafted a plan to reach thousands through the Montgomery family...through Crew Cutless?

And what if the enemy, upon seeing that grand plan begin to unfold, sought to steal, kill, and destroy that plan?

Such were the thoughts running through the mind of the gentle soul, playing out in the form of pictures in the deep recesses of unconsciousness, where visions are often birthed. He'd lulled off to sleep cradling his old, worn Bible while preparing for Sunday's message. He awoke with a start:

"Jeannie!"

His wife, busy unloading clothes from the dryer, hurried out to her husband. She'd been married to him for more years than she cared to think about and knew he never interrupted his Bible-study time.

"What is it, honey? Is somethin' wrong?"

"I'm not sure. I dozed off sittin' here studying and had a strange dream that's made me feel unsettled. You know where scripture says whenever two or more are gathered in prayer, the Lord joins 'em?"

"Are you looking for a partner?"

"Looks like it. I don't know what we're s'posed to pray for, other than it has to do with the Montgomery family and maybe Crew. Wouldja kneel down here with me and just let the Holy Spirit intercede for us?"

"Lord knows we've done it plenty of times before...we'll just be open vessels, and hopefully the Spirit'll do the rest." Jeannie used the pastor's shoulder to brace herself as she worked to get down on the floor beside him. Her knees made an awful popping sound. She laughed. "This old body sure ain't what it used to be."

"I love you just the same," Preacher Walker replied warmly. "Just the same as the day you were crazy enough to say 'I do' to a country boy who didn't even have two nickels to rub together."

"All right, you don't have to get all sentimental on me; we're rich now, at least where it matters. Let's get to prayin'."

They knelt on the floor together, hand in hand, until they could no longer feel their legs and their feet tingled. Every once in a while, one of them would feel impressed to speak a verse or two of scripture out loud or to hum a chorus from an old hymn, but other than that, the room was quiet. Behind them was the angel who had been in Miss Charity's room earlier that morning. Neither could see or feel his presence. His large, muscular hands rested on their shoulders as he bent over them and breathed two words: "Miss Charity." A tear escaped one of his eyes, making a wavy path down his dark, smooth cheek. He didn't catch it.

Jeannie suddenly felt impressed to speak a name out loud: "Miss Charity."

The pastor joined in agreement: "Yes, Lord, protect our sweet angel, Miss Charity. Oh, how we love that little gal."

After the angel heard her name, he was gone. Mission accomplished.

Later that night, the old preacher still couldn't concentrate. Making notes on points he wanted to make in his next sermon, he shuffled through his trusted notebook. Thoughts continued to make war in his mind.

What if you are part of the plan? My plan?

What if you and Jeannie were placed in Mary's life when she was just a little thing, because some day you would be needed to call down the heavens for her sake?

What if Crew is both good and evil? Still lost and yet found?

And what if Miss Charity's disability...

Jeannie peeped in and interrupted his thoughts: "Hey, could I get you a cup of coffee to help you stay awake?"

"Nah, I think I'll just put all this stuff away for the night and hit the sack; I can't think straight tonight for nothin'."

"Still feelin' uneasy?"

"Yep, still as uneasy as a fly who's bein' chased by a swatter. It beats all."

Preacher Walker and Jeannie climbed into bed and turned out the lights. The Lemon Drop Party was now in full swing. A group of police officers had managed to park their cars down the street and out of sight from Crew's house without being noticed. They were waiting on the signal from the lead officer before surrounding the house and cutting off all routes of escape for an estimated thirty teenagers.

"There could be more," one said.

"It's going to be a long night for a lot of parents," answered another.

Chapter 13

Wills looked at the time.

"Hey, Tater, help me clean up the kitchen so we can get that movie started."

"Why are you in such a hurry? Mom and Dad won't be here 'til late."

"Let's just say I've got some things that have to be done tonight." Wills was talking to Tate but appeared to be partially talking to himself as well. "Yep, tonight is an important night," he rambled.

His sisters were fed, the kitchen was clean, and now Tate busily hunted for the video she wanted to watch.

"Found it!" she hollered from the storage closet.

Tate slid on the wooden floors into the great room with her sock feet, DVD tightly in hand, pretending to be an ice skater who'd come in for a final bow after completing a perfect performance.

"Thank you so much." She blew kisses to her audience of two. Wills was standing by the TV, waiting on the DVD.

"Did you see that, Wills? I bet I slid two feet or more and didn't come close to falling." She was so excited about spending time with her brother and didn't try to hide it.

Wills, however, wasn't in the mood for her antics. "How about cutting the drama and handing me the DVD!"

His words stung; her face prominently displayed it for Wills to see.

"Wow, your mood sure has changed." She handed him the DVD. "Me-ow...hiss, hiss!" She walked away acting like an angry cat, clawing at the air, poking fun at her brother.

Wills, realizing he'd probably been too gruff, had to think quick to get the evening back on the right track. On his track. So at once, he dropped to his knees and started barking like a dog, crawling all around the floor: "Woof! Woof! Woof!" He was now, for all intents and purposes, a dog chasing the hissing cat. And before the girls knew what hit them, he had knocked Tate onto the couch, face first, next to Miss Charity, and was tickling them both. Tate jumped into the act, forgetting she was supposed to be mad. She was quite the actress, meowing loudly as she giggled. Miss Charity, not fully understanding the barking and the meowing, enjoyed every minute of the hullabaloo. She stuck one of her feet out toward Wills so he'd be sure to tickle it.

"All right, girls, what do you say we get that movie started?" he suggested, abruptly cutting the performance short.

Tate protested: "No Movie! More tickling! Meow! Meow!"

Miss Charity kept dangling her little feet in front of him, daring him to tickle them again. Instead, he became the dog again, grasped her foot, and acted like he was going to chew on her toes.

"I'm gonna eat me a toe sandwich," he shouted. She pulled her feet back, laughing out loud, trying to save her feet from the brother who was acting so funny.

"That's right, Miss, if you put your toes out here, I'll gobble them up!" Wills teased. He gave the little one a kiss on her cheek and a pat on her head before jumping up to start the DVD.

"Sulley and Mike crack me up; I can't wait to see this movie again." Tate was sitting on the couch, already wrapping up in a fuzzy blanket, with Miss Charity cuddled up close beside her. She felt so happy inside. Wills inserted the DVD, pushed play, and took a seat on the ottoman in front of Tate.

"Hey, if you sit in front of me, how am I gonna watch the movie? Move it, puppy dog!" Tate gave her big brother a playful shove, but he didn't budge.

"Tate, I need to ask you something."

His voice was serious.

"Really? Well, can you pause the movie so I don't miss anything?"

"Just hear me out; it won't take a second. I need you to do a super-huge favor for me."

Tate loved the idea of doing a favor for her big brother.

"Sure, what's up?"

"Before I tell you, I need you to promise me you will keep a secret."

"OK...I can keep a secret."

"Cross your heart and pinky swear?"

"I'm eleven now, so I think I'm a little old for that, don't you?"

Wills gave her an affirming grin. "Of course you are, and I know I can trust you. Crew's in trouble. I think he needs me."

"Should we call Mom and Dad?"

"No, this is something I can take care of without bothering them...and that's where the secret comes in. No matter what, you can't tell Mom and Dad about this. If you do, you'll break the brother-sister code."

"I can't tell Mom and Dad about what?"

"You can't tell them that I left you here in charge of Miss while I went to help Crew."

"Stay here by myself? In charge of Miss Charity? I can't do that!"

"I wouldn't ask you if it wasn't an emergency. I'm afraid Crew is getting ready to make a huge mistake."

Tate went from the eager sister, excited to do her brother a favor, to a little girl, completely afraid of being by herself and equally reluctant to disappoint the one she adored.

"But you know I'm scared to stay here by myself."

"You won't be alone...look, Miss Charity is here with you."

Tate looked over at her little sister, propped up on the couch and chewing on the end of one of Philip's athletic socks she'd snatched when someone left the laundry-room door open. Realizing Tate was gawking at her, she looked away from the movie long enough to give both Tate and Wills a half smile, but then she went right back to watching the movie.

"Uhhm, she's chewing a sock, Wills. How much help would she really be if a burglar came in with a gun to shoot us?"

"Tater, a lot of girls start babysitting when they are twelve, and you're nearly there. It's time for you to start taking more responsibility. Even if Mom and Dad can't see it, I know you're ready for this."

She took a few seconds to look at her brother's face and could tell he wanted her to do this...maybe needed her to do this. The next question was a difficult one for her to voice.

"How long will you be gone?"

Wills answered fast, before she had a chance to change her mind.

"Twenty minutes, tops. I'll be back so quick you won't even realize I've been gone."

He was already in motion, grabbing his coat from the kitchen counter.

"Just sit here with Miss and watch the movie; I guarantee you won't be scared."

Tate looked over at the little munchkin; the sock was soggy and wrapped around her little hand.

"Do you really think I'm ready for this?"

Wills was already on his way toward the door.

"You've got this, Sweet Po-Tater!"

"Twenty minutes, tops?" she asked, hoping.

"Twenty minutes, tops...I'll even set the timer on the oven for you. If it goes off and I'm not back, just call me on my cell phone, and I'll talk to you until I'm back in the house."

And with those final words, he closed the door and took off in a sprint.

Since Crew lived nearby, in the same historic area of Cleveland, he figured it would take him less than five minutes to get to his house. He checked his cell phone as he ran but found no reply to the texts he'd sent Crew. It was nearly seven thirty, so by his estimation, everyone should have already arrived at the party. He made a mental note to be home by seven fifty.

The heavy breathing surprised him. Listening to one foot fall before the other, hitting the cold, hard ground, he forced his legs to keep moving. After spending two weeks in bed, his body cried out for him to stop.

"Twenty minutes is all you've got. You can do this. Just gotta keep moving."

When he arrived at the basement door, Wills checked his cell phone for the time again. It was 7:37 p.m. It had taken him longer than expected. He had only ten minutes to find Crew and get him to stop the party. He didn't want to make a scene, so he'd have to act like he normally did...he would be his same old friendly self and blend in until he found Crew. Then, he'd ask him to come outside to talk to him. To convince him. And Crew would listen.

A shiver went up his body as he made a final move toward the door. For a split second, terror nearly paralyzed him. Two words flooded his mind: "Miss Charity." He almost gave in to the sudden onslaught of fear welling up inside him, but instead, he pushed it all down, took a deep breath, and turned the handle. Within moments, he was being greeted by familiar faces who appeared sincerely happy to see him. One shook his hand. "Hey, everybody, look who's back!"

A fellow football player gave him a bear hug. "Man, it's good to see you on your feet again!"

"I didn't expect to see you here!" shouted someone else.

He didn't realize how much he'd missed his friends. It felt good to be welcomed back...to be part of the group again. He made the rounds for a few minutes, catching up on the latest happenings and gossip. Sights captured his eyes, luring him in. It never ceased to amaze him how a girl he barely noticed at school could become irresistible when missing the majority of her clothing.

"Looking good tonight, ladies," he spoke to a small group of girls as he passed by. One of them reached out and grabbed him for a hug. He hugged her back, tight, noticing how she pressed her body against his. It was intentional; they both knew it, so he lingered in the hug before walking away.

Thoughts punched him in the gut: *What are you doing, Wills?*

His senses were now in overdrive. This was going to be much more difficult than he expected. Another thought: *Get out!*

But scents intoxicated him, daring him to explore their origins. The same girl he'd just sensually embraced decided to go in for another round with Wills. As he walked away, she followed and wrapped her arms around his waist from behind. He couldn't resist. He didn't even try to resist. Pulling her around to face him, he breathed her in. She smelled like a mix of beer and perfume. She gave him an unspoken invitation with her eyes, so he kissed her. The party around him stopped for a moment while he melted with this girl. He didn't know her that well at all, but it didn't matter. That was what a Lemon Drop Party was all about. No commitments. No promises. No ties. And no holds barred.

His mind wandered and found another thought: *Go home.*

He pushed the thought out of his mind while simultaneously pushing the girl away from him.

"Not now, baby, but I'll find you later, OK?"

In response, she grabbed the back of his head, allowed her fingers to lock around his hair, and pulled him close to her face.

"Don't forget me," she muttered. A little more than tipsy, her voice dripped with flirtation. "You're all mine tonight."

After one last kiss, she sauntered away with confidence, knowing he'd find her again.

Wills knew where to find the party's host. He made his way toward Crew's bedroom, just off the main party area. As he expected, a group of guys were standing around watching a large flat-screen mounted on the wall.

Crew spotted him immediately.

"Hey, Preacher Boy! I wondered when you'd show up."

Once again, a barrage of thoughts came. This time they swept in like a flood, threatening to drown Wills if he didn't get out of the room.

Don't look at the TV.

You have to get back home.

Check the time.

You only have twenty minutes.

But instead of saving himself, Wills made the choice to drown.

"Hey, bro." Then, looking toward the others while reaching out to shake a couple of hands, he said, "Hey guys." Wills knew he shouldn't, but he couldn't keep himself from looking toward the TV. And once he gave that flat-screen the first glance, he was a goner. His plan to stop the party, to save Crew, was over.

To say evil is powerful would be a foolish understatement. Evil is a masterful seductress, with immeasurable experience, who will stoop to any level to get what she wants. At eight o'clock, the sound of policemen breaking through the door broke her spell.

"Oh, God! I've got to get home!"

Wills managed to check his phone before the police took it along with everyone else's. Sitting on the floor, surrounded by his peers, he felt horrible that he hadn't answered Tate's texts and calls. All he could do was hang his head in shock, feeling sick to his stomach for letting everyone in his life down. Again.

In the cacophony of sounds all around him...the police officers trying to calm everyone down...teenage boys and girls crying, cursing, and in a panic...Wills heard a familiar voice lacking all emotion:

"Hey, Preacher Boy, while we're all sitting here waiting to see if the cops can get through to my crazy mom upstairs, why don't you teach us all about Jesus?"

It was Crew.

Chapter 14

Miss Charity had Down syndrome and was nonverbal, but it would be a mistake to ever underestimate her abilities. She sat on the couch, chewing on her dad's sock while pretending to be caught up in the video, but all the time the wheels in her mind were turning. It might not be too much of a stretch to say she was formulating a plan. That little somebody fully understood what her big brother was about to do. He would be leaving her alone with Tate, and to the littlest munchkin in the Montgomery family, Tate was not an older sister but an equal. So, as soon as Wills sprinted out the door, she went to work.

First, she darted into the kitchen, opened a drawer full of baking pans, and threw them onto the floor. The loud, clanging racket sent stimuli to her brain as addictive as a heavy narcotic. Her brain begged her for more.

"Miss Charity, stop that right now!" Tate reluctantly left her movie to put the pans away. She noticed the laundry-room door had been left ajar as she was closing the drawer.

"Please tell me Wills did not leave that door open again." Marching in, as she feared, Tate found her little sister bent over a laundry basket, throwing all sorts of clothing over her shoulder as fast as her hands could move.

Socks, shirts, underwear, and pants were being strewn everywhere. It could have been the colors...or possibly the varying textures...who knew what drew the little spark plug to create such total disarray? The five-year-old grasped each piece of fabric with glee before randomly tossing it. The ease with which it all flew up in the air from the motion of her own hands seemed remarkable to Miss. And the fact that she had instigated the massive gob of garments was not lost on the tiny one. For her, it represented achievement. And Tate's reaction, the screaming and the show of impatience, was simply scrumptious icing on the proverbial cake.

"Stop it!" Tate fussed. But the impetus was too much. Miss wasn't about to stop.

The cutie with the ringlet-curled pigtail and rosy-rimmed glasses scampered past her sister from the laundry room, making a beeline back for the kitchen. Opening a drawer filled with shiny silverware with a yank that should have torn it clear from the cabinet, she snapped up handfuls and ferociously threw it all. Knives, forks, and spoons crashed onto the floor and the countertops. What would have been an earsplitting sound to most was sheer bliss to the ears of the one bearing the extra chromosome. At one point, becoming so laced with adrenaline, she stopped to bang her hands on the countertops while executing an outrageous, gruff, throaty noise rivaling that of a lion.

"What was that?" Tate answered the call of the wild while still doing her best to tidy the laundry room. If she could have seen her sister at that moment, she would have seen a little girl so pleased with herself...the untamed queen of the jungle successfully conquering her wasteland.

Tate peeked into the kitchen and was quick to accept defeat. There was no way to subdue the big cat holed up in the little body. As soon as she cleaned up one mess, Miss was already busy making another. Within a short span of time, the five-year-old had climbed on top of the kitchen table, climbed into an empty fireplace, jumped up and down on her parents' bed, stuffed a throw pillow into the toilet, and pulled a roll of toilet paper from the guest bath all the way through the house. Miss Charity was a textbook picture of a little girl whose senses were running high; her body craved it, so she eagerly indulged. Philip and Mary could have stopped her, Wills could have stopped her, but the little girl knew Tate didn't have a chance.

"I give up! Do you hear me? I give up!" Tate finally fell onto the couch, began watching her movie again, and ignored the behavior.

"Wills will have to clean all this up when he gets home, because I'm not going to do it anymore!" she protested. "He's the one who's supposed to be in charge...not me!" Miss Charity continued to wreak havoc on the old house while Tate watched her movie, until a crashing sound brought everything to a halt.

"Nooooo, what have you done now?"

Tate stomped her way toward the front entry of the home, blood boiling like a volcano about to erupt. She caught a glimpse of glass shattered all over the floor; but as usual, the guilty suspect had already fled the scene of the crime.

"You're going to be in big trouble for this one! Momma's granddaddy bought her this frame as a wedding gift, and it was special to her!" Tate preached, knowing no one was listening.

She rounded up a broom to sweep the remains of the glass from the picture frame that had displayed her parents' wedding photo for nearly twenty years. Carefully salvaging the paper photo, she placed it high up on a nearby shelf where Miss Charity couldn't get to it. She then dumped the glass into the garbage can, put the broom away, and noticed the house had become unusually quiet. She could hear the movie still playing in the other room, but she couldn't hear Miss Charity's feet bounding about. Feeling a tinge of worry, Tate walked through the house looking for her.

"Where are you, Miss Charity?"

She searched every room on the main floor. Miss Charity, afraid of the steps, never went upstairs without a hand to hold. But feeling unsure, Tate ran up the stairs to take a look. The lights were out, and there was no sign her sister had been up there, so she went back downstairs to continue the search.

"Miss Charity, this isn't funny!" she called while running back down the steps. "I'd rather you throw the silverware and the baking pans than hide from me..."

Panic settled in quickly.

"Jesus, please help me find my sister! Please, Jesus!"

Due to something the speech and occupational therapists called hyposensitivity, Miss Charity routinely chewed on things—on anything, in fact, that would fit into her mouth—as a way to feel and explore them. Tate's primary concern was that an object had accidentally become lodged in her throat. It happened way too often. Now dashing through the house, she hysterically called for her sister.

The oven beeped.

"Thank You, Jesus! Wills will be home any second." Grabbing the house phone, she called him while continuing to frantically look through the house for Miss Charity. He didn't answer. She sent him a text from her cell phone—still no answer.

"Miss Charity, this is not funny...please let me know where you are!" Tate started to cry. After trying to contact Wills several times with no answer, she broke the brother-sister code and called her mom.

"I'm sure everything is all right, Tate. Just keep on talking to me while you look for her..."

After receiving the call from home, Mary and Philip did not take the time to cancel their order with their waiter. Philip threw down plenty of cash to cover their meal, and they sprinted out to the car.

"Dad and I should be there in about ten minutes, OK?"

Mary's voice was cool and calm, even though she was furious with Wills for leaving Tate and Miss Charity alone.

"Have you checked under the beds, behind the clothes hanging in the closets, and behind all the furniture?"

"I looked in your closet, but not behind the clothes. I'll do that right now." Tate took off running for the closet.

"OK, beautiful girl, keep talking to me while you look for her; we're almost home now." Mary could tell Tate was beside herself with worry and did her best to soothe her while at the same time making sure she helped her find Miss Charity. Philip reached his hand over to hold Mary's as they drove on. She abruptly pulled it away from him.

Tate checked the closet in her parents' room first. She got down on her hands and knees, running her hands along the floor, underneath the hanging clothes, hoping to find a set of feet.

"She's not in your closet, Mom."

"Go in the bedroom and check under the bed."

Leaving the closet behind her, Tate passed through the master bathroom and entered the bedroom by way of a set of tall double doors. Tate couldn't audibly hear the invisible angel in the room, but she instinctively turned when he fondly spoke the words: "Miss Charity."

"I see her! Miss Charity, come out of there!"

"Oh, thank God! Where is she, Tate?" Mary asked.

"I think she's stuck, Momma. She's behind that old, wooden chest in your room, and she's not coming out," Tate answered her mom, but she continued to talk to Miss Charity as well: "It's all right, girl, come on out."

"Tate, is she breathing?"

That might have been an unusual question for most families, but not for the Montgomerys, who had dealt with Miss Charity's heart-defect issues her entire life.

"Yes, ma'am, she's breathing. She's just got her shoulders stuck in there, and she can't get loose.

I'm trying my best to pull her out, but she's really stuck bad."

"Don't hurt her, baby. Maybe you should just sit there with her and keep her calm until we get there."

Mary could hear Tate crying out loud.

"What's wrong, Tater Bug?"

"She's just looking at me like she doesn't understand why I'm not helping her get out; I can tell she's so scared."

"Well, I think you're both scared. Why don't you hold her hand and sing a song to her?"

"Do you think that will help?"

"I know it will help."

"What should I sing?"

"Sing 'This Little Light of Mine'...she'll love it!"

Mary pressed the cell phone as close to her ear as she could get it. If it were possible, she would have crawled through the phone into the room with her babies. She and Philip raced to get home, and as they raced, Mary mentally consumed the most beautiful rendition of "This Little Light of Mine" she had ever heard. The momma of three listened as Tate sang the song from her heart, one little girl doing her best to comfort another. Love on display for no other human on earth to see. For Mary's ears.

Tate held one of her sister's little hands while the unseen angel held the other.

"She smiled at me, Momma!"

"See there, Tate? She knows you're trying to help her. Just keep singing."

When Philip and Mary arrived, they were able to pull the antique wooden chest away from the wall and free the trapped Miss Charity, who now looked more like a harmless kitten than a fierce lion.

Mary knelt on the floor to be at eye level with her baby girl.

"Oh my word, Tate, what is all over her? Is it poop or chocolate?"

With Miss Charity, either was a good guess. At some point in the rampage, Miss Charity had found chocolate. Lots of it. From head to toe, she was smeared in the sweet confection that time had turned to brown crust. Mary held her shoulders and gave her a good look.

"Well, she seems fine, but she definitely needs a good bubble bath." She kissed the chocolate-covered face, giving a tickle up under her arms. Miss Charity threw her arms around her mother, knocking her to the floor on her back. Mary lay on the floor, holding her baby tight.

Tate, feeling blanketed by sweet relief following the chaos, looked at the two and answered with a laugh: "Just wait until you see what Miss Charity has been up to while you were away...this whole house may need a good bath."

Mary looked at the chocolate-covered face. "How could someone so cute get into so much trouble?"

Tate filled Mary in on all of Miss Charity's mischief while she ran the warm bathwater into the claw-foot tub. Miss Charity stood by, wearing only a diaper, anxiously waiting to be scrubbed down. She loved baths. For her, the tub was a small version of a swimming pool.

Philip came in just as the little one lay on her stomach in the bubbles and started to kick. Water splashed all over the place.

"Well, look at you swimming!"

Little Bit looked up at her daddy, so pleased with herself. He was the one who had taught her to kick her feet in the water. But his real intent for coming into the bathroom was to talk to Mary.

"I'm going to Crew's house and will hopefully bring Wills back home in one piece; I hope I don't have to drag him home."

Mary refused to look his way. "This is your cross to bear, Philip, so you better do something. I told you we should break up that friendship, but you wouldn't listen to me..." She spoke while giving

Miss Charity a good scrub and continued her rant as Philip tried to duck out the bathroom door. "You wanted us to bring Crew into our home? Into our home! Wills is still recovering from a concussion, and he's out at one of those Lemon Drop Parties that gave him the concussion in the first place..."

In all the evening's drama, Mary had forgotten about her early-morning meeting with Viv. When she heard herself say "Lemon Drop Parties" out loud, her sister's information suddenly dawned on her.

"Oh, Lord, Chief! You have to get in the car and get over there as fast as you can! Viv came by this morning and told me the police are going to raid that party tonight. Go! Get out of here *now!*"

Mary stood up from the bathtub and started pushing Philip out the bathroom door and through the master bedroom. He tried to process what she was saying. "What? The police..."

"There's no time! Get out of here and get Wills *now!* Call me from the car on your way over there...*hurry!*"

Philip raced to his car, threw it into reverse, and sped out of the driveway...much as he had the last time Wills attended a Lemon Drop Party. He called Mary from his cell phone on the way.

"OK, what do you mean, the police are going to raid the party?"

"Viv came by the house early this morning when I was doing my Bible study. She came to tell me Crew was having another party and that the police were onto it. According to her boyfriend, the entire police force is coming out tonight."

"Why didn't you give me this information this morning so I could have stopped Crew from having the party?"

"Because I wanted him to get caught; I thought it would be a good lesson for him."

"I'm almost there...just pray I get Wills out before the police get to him."

Philip hung up without saying good-bye. Mary didn't care. She went back to bathing the little beauty.

"Thanks to your dad, Wills may be having his birthday party in the slammer this year!"

Chapter 15

Seeing both the outdoor and indoor lights shining at Crew's house provided Philip with his first clue. He was definitely walking into trouble. The all-too-familiar car parked along the curb outside of Crew's house offered the second one.

"GiGi and Poppy. What in the world are they doing here?" he mumbled while locking the car and making his way to the basement door.

The number of teenage kids didn't surprise him. But the number of police officers and parents absolutely took him aback. It didn't take him long to spot the one set of grandparents, his son's grandparents, standing right next to Wills, looking chagrined.

"Lord, Poppy, we're caught dead to rights!" GiGi tried to speak like a ventriloquist, without moving her mouth. She hoped Philip wouldn't see what she was saying. It didn't work. He read her lips along with her body language; she projected sheer panic.

After taking several long strides forward to meet him halfway in the overcrowded room, Mary's mother grabbed Philip by the arm and spoke in hushed tones, as if everyone around them would be trying to hear their conversation.

"Philip, Pops and I have got this whole thing worked out, so don't worry."

"Worked out? I don't even know what's going on!" he answered.

"Well, of course you don't, because that sweet Wills didn't want to worry you and Mary. He called us, and we came right over and fixed everything."

"Fixed everything?"

"Honey, Wills was over here trying to convert all these souls to Jesus. He told us himself he came over to stop this party and to bring Crew back to his senses. He's such a special boy."

"A special boy? How can you say that? He left Miss Charity and Tate all alone in the house tonight, didn't bother filling Mary in on his devious plans, and Miss Charity got stuck behind the chest of drawers in our bedroom. What if her heart had given out on her...or what if she'd suffocated?"

"Oh, dear, I didn't know about that...is our baby OK?" GiGi was instantly concerned.

"Yeah, she's OK...thankfully. But she could've been hurt badly tonight...or worse."

"Well, nothing bad happened, Philip. God's protecting her. And Wills made a mistake, but he is still a child and is so sorry."

"A child? The police sure aren't acting like this is a bunch of harmless child's play."

Philip pulled away from his mother-in-law and pushed on straight for Wills, who was still standing next to Poppy. The boy and his grandfather both looked like a couple of deer caught in a set of headlights. Poppy, ever the defender, wrapped his arm around Wills's waist and gave him a squeeze.

"Don't you worry, Wills; GiGi and I are going to stand right with you on this." Poppy's voice was a bit shaky. He was nervous about the entire situation.

As for GiGi, she wasn't one to give up that easy. Walking right along beside Philip, step for step, she was determined to talk him down before he reached Wills.

"You know, Philip, nobody's perfect. Just keep in mind that you were a teenager once too...and..."

"Please, GiGi, don't talk to me anymore about this until I've had a chance to speak with *your* grandson." His message to her couldn't have been clearer.

GiGi allowed Philip to take a step past her so she could silently mouth necessary words of warning to Wills and Poppy once she was safely behind his back. "You" (she pointed her finger rapidly at Wills) "are in big trouble" (and then she made a very large circle using both her hands before pounding one fist into the palm of her other hand with a loud thump to make her point).

She then drove the point home further by flashing big, wide eyes toward her grandson and giving him an exaggerated shrug, nonverbally stating she'd failed at getting through to him. Her efforts, although valiant, had been in vain.

But just before Philip made his way around the throng of teenagers and through the sea of parents speaking with police officers, he heard his name being called:

"Mr. Montgomery!"

He had been fixed on getting to Wills, but he instinctively followed the sound of his name. It was the fair-haired boy sitting in a chair in a corner of the room. No parents around him. No friends around him. He was alone. Crew motioned for Philip to come over to him.

Philip gave a quick glance back at Wills, who had his grandfather by his side, and made a split-second decision to go to Crew. But he first gave his son a warning: "I'll deal with you in a second! Stay right there and don't move, or else!" Philip literally shouted the words at Wills before making the turn to go to the one who seemed to need him most.

Wills recoiled back into his grandfather's shoulder: "Lord, Poppy, I'm as good as dead."

GiGi, seizing the opportunity, masterfully weaved and bobbed around the multitude like an acrobat, reaching Wills and Poppy in an instant. She was out of breath.

"Let's go. Thank the Lord for parting the Red Sea and allowing a big old wave to carry Philip on over to Crew. We've signed the papers already, so let's get the heck out of this God-forsaken basement. The land is dry before us; let's get out while the getting is still good!"

"But, GiGi, did you not just see and hear Dad? He told me to stay here."

"If you want to remain in one piece, you'll listen to me." She grabbed his arm and started pulling him along with her toward the exit. "Your dad looks mad enough to rip your fanny clear off your body, stomp on it, chew it up, and then spit it out. Now, come on, let's hightail it out of here while we've got the chance and while your booty is still intact!"

Wills looked to his grandfather for advice. "Poppy, Dad will kill me if I leave."

Poppy took his other arm and joined GiGi in the effort to get Wills out of Crew's basement. "She's right. I've never seen your dad look so angry, bud. Let's listen to your GiGi for once and get out of here while the gettin' is still good."

"Wills, think about it, honey." GiGi was pretty much dragging her one and only grandson at this point. "He's going to kill you either way! A killin' is a killin', and it's a-comin' to you no matter what. Our leaving is only buying you a little more time. Now quit resisting and come on!"

On the way out the door, GiGi felt compelled to thank one of the officers while handing him a form she'd signed for Wills.

"Y'all have done such a lovely job this evening, Officer. My grandson was here trying to lead all these hoodlums away from sin tonight. You know how it is, being caught at the wrong place at the wrong time." She smiled, pleased with her defense of Wills. "Please don't hold it against him, all right? He's been baptized and belongs to Jesus."

The police officer took the form, nodded, and went back to the conversation he was having with another family.

While exiting the door, she hustled Poppy and Wills on outside before giving in to another urge to make an announcement to the swarm of people gathered in the room.

"You teenagers need to find Jesus." Wagging her finger, she spoke with what she considered to be the authority of God. "The porno is going to take you all down unless you repent from that smut and ask for forgiveness!"

Philip heard her. The entire basement full of people heard her. GiGi was on her soapbox and feeling full of herself.

"Jesus saves! Hallelujah, Jesus saves! Give up the porno and hooch, and cling to the cross!"

Directing his attention away from Crew, toward the sound of his mother-in-law's irritatingly high-pitched voice, Philip was not happy to catch his son slipping out the door. "Porno," he repeated, "and hooch...she's a nutjob."

"So, Mr. Montgomery..." Crew drew him back to more important matters, which at the moment was himself. "My mom is passed out upstairs on meds, as usual, and my dad's probably not coming home for a few days or months or years." He gave a nervous chuckle. "I need someone to sign the paper for me."

"I'm sorry, Crew, but I'm still at a loss. What paper do you need me to sign?"

"The cops, they somehow found out about this party; they broke in here like this was an episode of *NCIS* and scared the ba-jeebies out of us." Crew rubbed his palms together.

Philip listened.

"We're kids, you know. They found beer, a couple of kids messing around, and some pornography, and you'd think the world was coming to an end. Even GiGi thinks we're all going to hell." Another nervous laugh.

Philip still didn't say a word.

"They came with these forms that have to be signed by parents. The forms say they won't take us to juvie and won't put this incident on our school records if we agree to do some community-service work and attend a seminar by the health department."

"And you need me to sign your form for you? To stand in for your parents?" Philip asked.

"Would you, sir? I don't want something like this going on my school record."

"Crew, I thought these parties stopped once Wills got hurt...and once you gave your heart to Jesus. Make fun of GiGi all you want, but to a certain extent, she's right. You all do need to repent and turn away from this junk."

"I know. And I have learned my lesson this time. I promise, sir. I just can't let this thing go on my record and ruin my chances to play college football. It was a stupid mistake, and I'm sorry."

Crew nervously watched Philip, ready to counter anything that came out of his mouth.

"If I sign this form, will you promise me you'll go to counseling with Preacher Walker for the next six weeks?"

"Yes, sir. I'll do anything. Counseling, cleaning the church, praying every day, you name it; literally, I'll do anything."

"I'm going to add the counseling to the form before I sign it...a little more praying wouldn't hurt you either...and I'm going to make you sign it, too."

"Of course, sir. Like I said, I'll do anything."

"Let me see if I can grab a police officer." He patted the boy on the shoulder. "I think we can fix all this."

After going over the form with an officer, Philip added the counseling sessions with Preacher Walker to it and signed it. The police officer, however, had one additional condition: "Mr. Montgomery, Crew is a minor, and as you can see, he's been drinking tonight. We couldn't get through to his mom, and his father never took our calls. So, bottom line, I can't accept the form from you unless you agree to take responsibility for him for the night...otherwise, he's headed to the Juvenile Detention Center. Is that all right with you, Crew? Will you agree to go home with Mr. Montgomery and not cause any more trouble?"

"What's up with his mother? I don't understand," Philip interjected.

"I'm not at liberty to discuss that with you, Mr. Montgomery. You've just got to trust me. The boy would be better off in juvie than to stay here in her care this evening. Will you take him or not?"

"Yeah, of course I will." He patted Crew on the back. "This boy is like a son to me."

"Well, everyone in this town wants Crew to succeed," the officer said, signing the form himself before turning his attention toward the young man standing at Philip's side, "but man, Crew, you've got to keep your feet on the straight and narrow, or you'll mess up all your chances at college football. Don't let that opportunity slip away from you...got that, son? This town is counting on big things from you and Wills; ain't that right, Mr. Montgomery?"

"That's right, Officer," Philip managed, shaking the man's hand.

"Boys will be boys, I reckon. But back in my day, my butt would've been kicked clear to the next county if I'd pulled a stunt like this," the policeman added, shaking his head as he walked away to deal with the next teenager.

Crew intentionally dropped his eyes toward the floor, visibly aggravated by the officer's remark. The most popular kid in town couldn't help but be reminded how no one cared about him as a person; it was always about football.

"Pack some things together, and let's get out of here, Crew." Philip encouraged Crew by giving him a slight hug around his shoulder.

"Is Mrs. Montgomery going to be all right with me staying at your house tonight?"

"Don't worry about that right now. Just do what I said; go get your things together."

Crew took off for his bedroom and began throwing clothing and toiletries into a duffel bag. A small part of him felt thankful Philip had come to the rescue, but the much greater part was full of burning fury. He hated that he'd been caught, despised being treated like a child. Crew hungered for revenge...revenge against Wills for being so sanctimonious, against the cops for acting like such big shots, and especially against the unlucky putz who had turned him in. That kid would pay.

As for Philip, there was no way he was taking the teenager to his house. As soon as Crew was out of sight, he dialed Preacher Walker's number.

"I hate to call you so late, but do you still have that room at your house made up for Crew?"

Chapter 16

It had been a long, long night for the Montgomery family. Philip, out until the wee hours of the morning, ended up taking much more time than he had planned to get Crew settled in at the pastor's house. When he did finally get home, to make a bad evening even worse, a pillow, a blanket, and a pair of pajama bottoms awaited him on the pullout sofa in the great room. Mary had made her intentions clear. At least Trudy welcomed him. She was snoring, curled up fast asleep next to Philip's pillow when he climbed in the makeshift bed to go to sleep. While Philip didn't sleep in the literal doghouse, he did sleep with the dog.

The morning sun was bright, following such a dark evening. It filtered through the blinds and summoned him to wake. Opening his eyes, he was caught a bit off guard when he found himself surrounded by Mary, GiGi, and Poppy.

"Rise and shine, Chief!" Mary growled, gritting her teeth.

Philip waited a few seconds for his eyes to adjust and then looked around the room. "Hey, guys, was this meeting on my schedule? If it was, I didn't get the memo." As usual, her husband made his best effort to ease the heaviness with humor, but of course, it didn't work. It never did.

"Did you get the memo about your son's birthday? Oh, and in case you've forgotten, I'm talking about your son, Wills, not your other son." Mary's heart raced as her blood pressure soared.

"Am I missing something?" Philip, groggy, tried to catch up with those in the room who appeared to have an agenda. So far, he was lost.

GiGi and Poppy, sitting on a nearby love seat wearing bathrobes, had obviously stayed the night. GiGi never missed an opportunity to say something. But not this morning. *Why so quiet?* he wondered.

"Right now, I wonder if you're missing your brain," his wife replied curtly just before Viv waltzed into the room, fully dressed, looking ready to tackle the day, with a cup of hot coffee already in hand.

"Good morning, all!" After the previous evening, she was feeling chipper, knowing all vibes would be directed at Philip for a while instead of her.

"Before we go on any further in this, um, meeting, are there any other guests who spent the night at the house?" Philip asked.

Viv, unlike her parents, was willing to speak up regardless of the tension. "Well, Philip, if you had come home sometime before three, you probably would have noticed our cars parked in the turnaround. But since you didn't...*surprise!*"

Viv didn't stop there.

"And because you weren't here last night for your family, GiGi, Poppy, and I had to step in and offer support on your behalf. Don't worry about saying thank you, though, because we know you're tickled pink to see us this morning."

Viv's sarcasm always wore on Philip's nerves, but on this already awkward morning, he wished he could tell her to shut up. A true southern gentleman, however, he always kept thoughts akin to those hidden safely in his head.

"Oh, Viv, you know he had to go spend half the night caring for his *other* son...never mind that his *own* son was in a panic, and Miss Charity was still shaken up from getting stuck behind the bureau. But there was no need for him to call us. Why would he do something considerate like that?" Mary was on a roll too.

Philip tried to think of what he could say to quench the flaming darts being hurled at him, but nothing came to mind. Mary had a problem with Crew, and it wasn't like the boy was going to disappear from their lives or go away. *Change the subject*, he thought.

"So, is everything set for Wills's birthday party?" Philip moved to sit up on the end of the sofa bed and face those gathered, setting his jaw and working to look more sure of himself.

The subject shift allowed GiGi the opportunity to break her silence.

"Viv picked up the cake and brought it over last night. Wills is going to love it, because it has his football number on it. And we've got everything we need to grill the burgers. I'm going to whip up some cinnamon rolls here in a minute for breakfast. Ooooh, we are going to make this the best birthday Wills has ever had!"

"Like that's gonna happen," Viv added under her breath, barely loud enough for everyone to hear, making GiGi furious.

"Yes, it will happen, Viv, so put a sock in that mouth of yours. Today is not about Mary, Philip, Crew, or you...it's about our precious Wills...and we're all gonna put on our big-girl and big-boy undies...and we're going to *make* this the best birthday Wills has ever had! You hear me? Everybody better straighten up and get it together!"

GiGi hopped up from the love seat and forged on to the kitchen with her nose up in the air. It was time to bake her cinnamon rolls.

"And with that little speech, I think I'll catch a shower." Philip quickly excused himself, making a speedy escape.

"Thanks for leaving us, you coward. Sure, we'll be more than happy to make up your bed!" Viv heckled Philip while rising to assist Mary in tucking the sofa bed away.

"Can you believe the nerve of him?" Mary asked her sister.

"He definitely has a soft spot for Crew. For what it's worth, I'm on your side on this one. That man's place last night was with his own family. Wills and Miss Charity...and even Tater Bug...needed their daddy."

Mary fluffed a pillow. "Is it wrong for me to hate Crew Cutless?"

GiGi overheard her from the kitchen and couldn't help but pontificate.

"Yes, Mary, it is wrong to hate Crew Cutless! The Bible says it's a sin!"

"I'm sorry...was I talking to you or Viv?" Mary shot back.

Poppy turned on the local news, ignoring the bickering. Nonconfrontational by nature, he felt uneasy when others argued or disagreed.

"I don't care whether you're talking to me or not; I'm your mother, and that gives me permission to tell you what I think, whether you want to hear it or not. And I get to do it for the rest of my life! The Bible says 'Thou shalt not hate,' so it is wrong for you to hate Crew Cutless! Period!" GiGi declared without taking a single breath, her words rolling off her tongue.

Viv jumped in with vigor: "The Bible doesn't say that! 'Thou shalt not hate' is not one of the Ten Commandments in *my* Bible."

"Did I say it was one of the Ten Commandments? Did I say that, Miss Know-It-All? No, I didn't. The Bible says to love your enemies, doesn't it? It's the same difference. I am glad of one thing, though, Viv...at least it sounds like you're reading your Bible. That's a first for you, isn't it?"

"Look, I'm not feeling up for one of your sermons, Mom, and I think we're upsetting Pops." Mary plopped down on the couch, mentally exhausted after a long night.

"Are you kidding me?" GiGi shot back. "I tried to tell all of you Wills was probably into the porno, but none of you took me seriously. Now God only knows what that precious boy has seen. He no longer has the virgin eyes, and he certainly won't be able to unsee it all now, will he?"

She continued the lecture.

"And, Viv, I'm warning you; your life is looking too much like that crazy TV show about the bachelorette. You go through guys like the kids in this family go through bottles of ketchup. If you don't pipe it down a few notches, people are going to start getting the wrong idea, 'cause I'm your momma, and I'm starting to get the wrong idea! And as for you, Mary..."

"Please, Mom, I'm telling you; it's been a long night." Mary closed her eyes and made an earnest plea, but it didn't work.

"You've had a long night? Hello? I think we've all had a long night, and you are going to hear me out. I never thought I'd say this, but you're just becoming plain old ill-tempered. This whole family is somehow becoming a hot mess, and if we're not careful, Jesus just might give us all a whoopin'. There, now deal with some truth! Sermon over."

GiGi crammed the cinnamon rolls into the oven, set the timer for twenty minutes, and, feeling plenty peeved, called out to Poppy.

"Hey, Pops, let's go on upstairs and get dressed for the day before the kids wake up. At least they will be a joy to be around today!"

Poppy rose from the love seat, sauntered sheepishly over toward his daughters, and gave them each a soft kiss on top of their heads. He then followed the boss up the stairs.

Mary and Viv sat quiet for a few minutes, making sure their mother was too occupied in the bedroom upstairs to hear them talking. But Viv couldn't contain her temper for very long.

"She makes me so mad! *The Bachelorette*? I wish I could get on that show and kiss every single one of those men right on the mouth just to irritate her." Viv grabbed a throw pillow and pretended to be kissing a man. "Momma, did you see that? I just kissed this handsome hunk of a man!" She then reached over and grabbed another pillow. "And did you catch that? I kissed this one's luscious lips right off his face!"

Mary couldn't contain herself; she guffawed at picturing her mother watching Viv on a show like that. "Well, at least you're not becoming ill-tempered. Lord knows why I would *ever* be ill-tempered, right?"

"Oh, sure, being ill-tempered is so much worse than being a tramp, which is obviously what I am since I go through men like bottles of ketchup." Viv rolled her eyes. "And she's one to judge, because Miss Prissy Pants is never ill-tempered, is she?"

Viv got up and started walking around the room, shaking her hips and strutting about like a peacock as she took each step, mocking her mother's high-pitched voice: "I'm telling you, Mary; Wills is into the porno! And I am now an expert on the porno because I watch the *Dr. Phil* show."

The sisters burst out in giggles, just like they had done their whole lives growing up together.

"Why do we have to have a momma who even knows about 'the porno'? I swear, Pops has to stop her from watching that *Dr. Phil* show, or she's gonna put us all in the nuthouse," Mary added.

"Put us there?" Viv gave a huff.

Both were enjoying talking about their mother a little too much. At least that was GiGi's opinion. She yelled from the hallway upstairs: "I may be old, but I'm not deaf! I know about the porno because I keep myself informed like every responsible US citizen should do."

The grandmother, who prided herself in working out at the gym every day of the week (except for the Lord's Day, of course), took off down the steps, ready to lay into her daughters. But just as she reached the bottom step, Tate came around the corner.

"Hey, Momma! I think something's wrong with Miss Charity. She won't get up!"

Tate had spent the night on the floor of her little sister's room, right next to her bed, because she had felt bad about the little one getting stuck behind the large chest while in her care. At some point in the night, Miss had crawled out of her toddler bed and snuggled up next to Tate. When Tate awoke, the little girl's big, brown eyes were looking straight at her. But she wouldn't move.

Mary, Viv, and GiGi followed Tate back to the bedroom.

"How's Momma's best girl this morning?" Mary glided into the room, still feeling so relieved her little angel had come out of the prior evening's activities unscathed. She wasn't worried at all; she just figured Miss Charity wasn't getting up because she was really tired from all the excitement the night before and was just not ready to get up yet.

Miss Charity didn't move. She didn't even respond to Mary with a smile. Instead, she lay flat on her back and only moved her eyes to look in her mother's direction.

They all realized something was very wrong.

Chapter 17

"She has a compression fracture in her back; I'm fairly certain it happened when she was trapped behind the chest in your bedroom last night." The emergency-room doctor delivered the news to an anxious family. "She's not moving because of the excruciating pain, and she might resist movement for several days. It's going to take a good six to eight weeks for her back to heal."

"Are there any special instructions on how we should handle her?" Mary asked.

"Yes, of course. Although I know it will be difficult, don't pick her up under her arms, and try to keep her from being too rambunctious. Our biggest concern is that she not reinjure it or make it worse."

"So no back brace?"

"A back brace wouldn't do any good, because she'd just wiggle out of it. I'll give you a prescription for pain meds, but other than that, her back is just going to need to take some time to heal on its own."

"All right, are we ready to go, then?" Philip was ready to get his little bundle of love back home, safe and sound, so he was disappointed when the doctor told him they'd have to stay at the hospital a little longer.

"Her cardiologist, Dr. King, was in today. When he saw Miss Charity's name up on the board, he stopped in to check on her. In the process of running tests to try to find why she was refusing to move, he suggested we check her heart. He wants to talk to you about that before you all get out of here."

GiGi couldn't help but blurt out, "Oh, Lord, is something wrong with her heart again?"

"I'm not a cardiologist, so I can't comment on that, but he should be by any minute. After your visit with him, you're free to go. It was nice meeting all of you today." The doctor shook everyone's hand and then moved on.

Philip, Mary, GiGi, and Poppy tried not to let their minds rush to full hysteria. The last cardiologist appointment had been just over six months ago, and the checkup was a positive one.

Tate had begged her parents to wait for her while she fetched Miss Charity's princess crown before they headed out to the hospital's emergency room in a rush. The crown now sat close beside her little head on the hospital bed.

"We're going to go home soon; you are such a brave princess." Poppy bent down and spoke softly in the patient's ear. In response, she looked up at her beloved grandfather with eyes full of adoration.

"That's my girl." Poppy kissed the top of her head and pulled away before she could see his tears fall. She looked so helpless lying there on the bed, unable to communicate her thoughts, fears, and feelings.

Dr. King breezed into the room wearing a shirt and tie. Upbeat and full of energy, he knew better than to wear a white coat around Miss Charity. He always talked and moved so fast. "How's my favorite patient?"

She still didn't move her body, but she strained her eyes around to look for the voice she immediately recognized.

"Hey, punkin pie! You found me! Now, can I listen to the fuzzy bunny rabbits hopping around in your chest for a second?"

The doctor pulled up Miss Charity's pajama shirt and listened carefully to her heartbeat. "Yep, those bunnies are still hopping around!"

Meanwhile, Mary could barely breathe. The thought of another heart surgery loomed in her mind, sneering at her, daring her to obsess. "Everything sounding all right, Dr. King?" She gave her best shot at keeping the quiver out of her voice.

"Well, would you look at that? Her angel is in the room." The doctor pulled his stethoscope away and stood for a minute, taking in the sight.

"You can see her angel?" Philip questioned.

The doctor, not wanting to interrupt the interaction between Miss Charity and her angel, kept his eyes on the little girl and spoke softly.

"I wish I could see it...but I don't need to see to know it's here. Look at how her eyes are looking to the left and how she's smiling. Her angel is probably playing pee-pie with her; maybe he's trying to keep her mind off of the pain. I see it often with my nonverbal patients, and it never gets old."

Everyone in the room watched closely, paying particularly close attention to the little patient's eyes. The room fell silent until her eyes finally moved to look at GiGi.

"Now she's looking at her angel," GiGi joked. Miss Charity gave a snort of laughter, as if understanding exactly what her grandmother had said.

"Your GiGi is silly, isn't she?" Poppy asked. Again, the little girl bearing the extra chromosome giggled, displaying a tiny dimple under the left side of her mouth. It was evident she loved her grandparents every bit as much as they loved her.

The cardiologist scratched his head, accidentally messing up the dark-brown hair that had been meticulously pulled back to form a neat, slick, low ponytail.

"She's got to be in a tremendous amount of pain with that compression fracture, but look at her work to keep everyone else happy and relaxed. She senses everyone is feeling worried about her." He lifted the blanket covering Miss Charity's feet and rubbed the hot-pink wool socks with his strong hands. Bringing his typically energetic voice down to a tender, calm level, he gazed into the little one's eyes.

"You're not an ordinary princess; did you know that? You are a great warrior princess, Miss Charity. I know you are feeling a whole lot of pain, and I bet you're even afraid. But you spend your time thinking of others, trying to put their minds at ease. You are so special, punkin pie."

He gave GiGi and Poppy half a grin with a wink. "Do you think you could take over my job and give this little gal a really good foot massage while I talk to Mary and Philip out in the hall?"

"Well, of course we can!" replied GiGi.

The doctor, walking away, reclaimed his typical vigor in giving one final directive to the grandparents.

"Now, I know it's going to be very tempting to tickle those cute little toes, but don't you dare do it, OK?"

Miss Charity heard Dr. King and reacted, bending her toes down tight and again giving a chuckle.

GiGi, happy to nurse her granddaughter back to health, responded, "It's not going to be me you have to worry about, Doc; it's this guy here who likes to tickle!" She gave her husband a jab with her elbow.

The doctor left the room with Mary and Philip. Poppy couldn't help himself. He kissed the tips of the sock-covered toes. "I do like to tickle those piggies an awful lot, GiGi, but not today. This girl can trust old Pops to take good care of her. Is that OK with you, Miss?"

Miss Charity relaxed her toes as Poppy grabbed one foot and GiGi took the other. The little princess enjoyed every second of their attention, not seeming to mind the absence of Mary and Philip at all.

"Poppy!" GiGi whispered, attempting not to move her mouth as she spoke.

"What are you doing? Miss Charity can hear you whispering, you know. You're much louder than you think you are!"

"It's not her I'm worried about." She looked around the room. "It's that angel. Do you think it's still flying around in here?" GiGi's eyes were wide with worry.

"I don't know, but I'm not gonna let it bother me. Mary and Tate have tried to tell us Miss Charity has an angel, so I reckon it's been verified today by the good doctor."

At some point during the foot massage, the little patient started to doze off.

"Look, Pops, she's going to sleep," GiGi whispered, still trying not to move her mouth for fear the angel might read her lips. "Once she's asleep, I hope that angel will flap its wings and get on out of here, don't you?"

They heard the sound of a kitten's purr; Miss Charity had given up her battle against the pain medication and was now being held captive in dreamland.

"Well, she's asleep, so I guess the angel has flapped its wings and left the building." Poppy flapped his arms up and down, moving his skinny legs like a chicken, poking fun at his wife.

The two grandparents, decked out in their matching preppy attire, took a seat in the sparse hospital room. "So you're honestly telling me you don't think the whole angel thing is creepy?" she asked.

"No, I don't think it's creepy. I hope I have an angel hangin' around me too."

"Why would you go putting that in my mind? I've never thought about an angel hovering around me every minute."

"You read the Bible and go to church every time the doors are open, but you've never learned about the angels?" Poppy looked at her like she was nuts.

She looked up and pointed at the ceiling. "Of course I've thought about God's angels; it would be sacrilegious not to accept all of His creation, but I always kind of pictured 'em up in heaven...flying around all happy with Jesus...not down here with me."

"And why is it a problem if an angel is down here with you flying around...all happy?"

"Well, now when I'm in the restroom or the shower...or trying on clothes in a department store...I'm going to be wondering if an angel is leering at me." GiGi shuddered at the thought, bugging her eyes out.

"The angel isn't creepy, but your thought process is very creepy. Why do you think an angel would want to see you sittin' on the pot?" Poppy got tickled thinking about his wife trying to hurry up and use the bathroom before an angel could catch her in the act. His eyes squinted when he laughed, and when he got started, it was hard to stop. He grabbed his belly and howled with laughter.

"This is not funny. I'm never going to be able to work my crossword puzzles on the throne again. From now on, I'll have to be in such a big hurry." GiGi was getting testier by the minute.

"Well, maybe you don't have an angel; have you considered that?"

"Oh, sure, like that will make me feel better." She sat for several seconds pondering the thought of not having an angel while Poppy did his best to muffle his laughter, being mindful not to wake Miss Charity. She broke the moment of silence with a huff: "So, do you think I have an angel or not?"

"If the good Lord thinks you need an angel, you'll have one. And if you do have one, I think it's probably a good-lookin' female angel who looks to be about sixty-five years old." Poppy was still laughing as he measured his wife's reaction. "And I bet she could compete with you at any crossword puzzle you threw her way."

"Well, I honestly didn't expect you to paint that picture for me."

"Yep. I thought that might getcha!"

"Thanks, honey." She patted his knee. "I think I'll be fine working my crossword puzzles in the bathroom now. I'll just look at it as an opportunity to show my angel how smart this old bird is. How dare she think she can take me on at a crossword puzzle; know what I mean? If I do have an angel, and I probably do, she better just worry about doing her job instead of trying to compete with the likes of me."

"I'm so happy you have me around to fix everything." Poppy pulled GiGi over to him and hugged her tight. "I'm picturing your angel in my mind right now; she sure is a pretty thing. And what do you know? She's given up her flowy white robe and is flapping all around us right now wearing the latest Ralph Lauren attire...probably a size six...maybe even a four."

GiGi pulled away from Poppy and folded her arms, pretending to be upset with him: "Now you've done it...you've taken it too far. My angel might beat me at crossword puzzles, but there's no way she can match this style." In an instant she was up prissing around the room doing turns and posing like a runway model. She even gave a beauty-queen wave. "Hello, crossword-working angel, give it up, because you don't want any of this!"

Poppy loved her spirit and sense of humor. His eyes squinted again as he laughed and laughed, trying to catch his breath.

In the corner of the room stood Miss Charity's angel, leaning against the wall. He, too, was laughing hysterically at the sight. Oh, how he wished GiGi's angel had been in the room to hear and see all he had just witnessed.

Chapter 18

Some changes showed up on Miss Charity's EKG when compared with the one that had been done six months earlier. Dr. King was slightly concerned but insisted that the parents not worry until they knew something more definite. "I'm completely optimistic," he'd said, attempting to put their minds at ease, but Mary was still a total wreck. His suggestion was that they bring the patient back in several weeks for an echocardiogram, which would hopefully provide a more in-depth look at the little girl's heart. Several weeks would feel like an eternity to her.

"They're home! Aunt Viv, let's get the food together!" Tate was the first to spot her family's Suburban rolling down Ocoee Street toward their home.

When the group reentered their home, it was early evening. They found Wills, Tate, and Viv ready to eat and have a proper birthday celebration. Viv and Wills had already grilled the burgers earlier in the day and had kept them warm in the oven. So, within a flash, all the food was set out family style on the old oak farmhouse table, ready to eat. After getting assistance from the pain meds, Miss Charity was feeling much better and took her usual place at the head of the table in her high chair. She began munching on a plate full of french fries, popping them into her mouth, one after another, barely chewing before swallowing. All the excitement, along with her long nap, had left her ravenous. In contrast, Mary, Philip, GiGi, and Poppy were beyond bone weary and not very hungry at all.

Philip led the blessing before they ate their meal. Plenty of carefree conversation about the food, the weather, and an upcoming charity auction followed, but Mary didn't have anything to say. She was fuming...feeling angry at Wills for putting Miss Charity and Tate in danger the night before, furious with her husband, who continued to make an effort to support the reprobate, Crew Cutless...but most of all, she was enraged at God for allowing her baby to be born not only with Down syndrome, sensory issues, and lack of communication skills, but also with a major heart defect. Miss Charity didn't get a one-two punch; she got a whopping one-two-three-four punch. Mary let herself drown in the injustice of it all. It wouldn't take much to set her off around the table; she silently dared anyone to mess with her. Fortunately for most of the family, her body language was easy to read. Too bad that wasn't the case with GiGi, who made an effort to break the ice.

"Wills, your Poppy and I couldn't be more proud to be your grandparents. We've discussed it and think you handled yourself responsibly last night. You went over to that party to lead those kids away from sin; your heart was in the right place, and that is what's most important. Things could've been a disaster, but here you are safe at home, celebrating your seventeenth birthday!"

Mary looked down at her plate, refusing to make eye contact with anyone. How dare her mother try to minimize the events? It was GiGi's way when it came to her family, especially her grandchildren. Dig a hole, dump the junk in it, cover it up, and forget it. Was it even possible for her to see?

GiGi rattled on, picking up the cadence of her spiel.

"And Philip, I want you to know I don't blame you one bit for reaching out to help Crew. That boy has been a part of our family for such a long time. We are all called to be more like Jesus, and sometimes we have to leave the ninety-nine sheep to go after that one little sheep that has gone astray. To me, you are like that picture that is hanging in our church...the one of Jesus carrying that cute little white lamb in His arms...you know the one I'm talking about, don't you? The Lord's wearing that flowy robe, and His hair is long with that full beard. By the way, while we're on the subject, are we even sure Jesus had long hair and a beard? I wish I could take a peek into heaven and see for myself, 'cause when I was growing up in the church, I was taught a proper Christian man keeps his hair neat and tidy and certainly doesn't wear facial hair."

Mary still managed to hold her tongue. Why was it obvious to everyone but her mother that she was in no mood for this type of "put the Band-Aid on the gaping wound" conversation, especially when her baby's health was now in question? Poppy was

sitting on the other side of the table, away from
GiGi, or he might have given her a gentle nudge, or
maybe even a stiff nudge, encouraging her to shut
up her crude display of diarrhea of the mouth. As
for Viv, she sat there grinning like a Cheshire cat
just waiting for World War III to unfold at any
moment. It was an ugly side to her. Other people
getting attention, either negative or positive,
meant her mother's attention was off of her. Every
fiber of Mary's being longed to launch a hamburger
bun at her sister's face, wiping the smile right off of
it. And as for her mother, she'd like to...

"Mary, I'm just going to put this out there,
honey..."

Mary's thoughts of revenge were cut off when she
heard her mother call out her name.

"Try to listen with an open heart, OK? Perhaps the
reason your family is going through such chaos is
because your heart isn't right with the Lord; have
you thought about that? Where is your
forgiveness? Why aren't you carrying that little
lamb in your arms? You have tossed Crew to the
curb, forced your husband to sleep on a pullout
sofa, and I haven't heard you say happy birthday to
your son one time since we got back home from
the hospital. The Bible says God won't forgive you
if you don't forgive others, so I think you might
need to think about letting it all go so God can start
answering your prayers. Who knows? Maybe he'll
even heal Miss Charity!"

That was it. It was either break down and cry or blow up, and there was no way on earth Mary was going to shed a tear, no way she would let her mother *or* God see even a sign of weakness in her.

"Get out of my house," she stated firmly, without raising her voice.

Philip spoke up: "Mary, you are hurting, but there is no reason to lose control and say things you'll later regret."

"Fine, I'll leave." Mary pushed herself from the table, stood up, took her keys, and left. Poppy followed behind her out the door.

"Hey, Mare-Bear, wait up for a second." In her entire life, there had never been a time her father couldn't get through to her, couldn't make things better, until now. She didn't stop. Starting the ignition, she placed the car in reverse and left. Poppy stood in the garage, watching her pull away.

"Oh, Father in heaven, protect my girl, and let her see You through all this chaos."

When he sat back down at the table, GiGi was busy telling everyone how Mary had overreacted and how she was just stressed about the cardiologist's report.

"She needs to take a drive and calm herself down. She'll pull it back together and will be just fine. Don't you worry, kids; your momma will be back in two shakes of a lamb's tail...like the one Jesus is carrying in that picture." She laughed out loud at her quick wit, but no one else joined in. Tate tried to be strong. She had been so worried about Wills lately and then had been worried about Miss Charity all morning and now was terribly concerned for her mother. Hadn't Mary always been the rock in the family? The one who took care of everyone?

"Daddy, is Mom gonna be all right?" she asked.

"Yes, Tater Bug, your GiGi is right. Momma just needs to take a drive and allow herself to calm down. The last few weeks have been tough for this whole family but especially your momma."

Wills felt horrible. In fact, he believed he had caused his mother's meltdown.

"This is all my fault. I'm sorry I ever met Crew."

"This isn't your fault, Wills." Viv enthusiastically offered her two cents on the subject. "GiGi sent your momma over the edge; she's been doing it to us since we were little girls."

"Why are you talking about me like I'm not sitting here at the table? I didn't send Mary over the edge; she just couldn't handle the truth. Neither of you have ever been able to deal with the truth." GiGi looked in Poppy's direction for confirmation. He said nothing and didn't even look her way.

"You're right, Momma. You do speak truth to us, but sometimes we don't need words or truth;

sometimes we just need some support," Viv argued.

GiGi should have taken Viv's words as a clue to change the subject. Perhaps she was overemotional after the long evening with Wills or maybe too tired to think straight after spending hours at the hospital. Whatever the reason, not only did she not stop the confrontation with Viv; she pursued it with a vengeance. In her eagerness to prove she was right, she left an unintended wake of destruction behind at the dinner table. Her voice, genteel and proper, was perfectly laced with her own unique version of a southern twang...so at once, *Gone with the Wind* meets *Coal Miner's Daughter* sliced, diced, and served Viv and Mary up on a silver platter. Philip, afraid of making things worse, said nothing. Poppy, on the other hand, tried to make side conversations with Tate and Wills, hoping they wouldn't hear half of what was being said. But they did hear. And although Miss Charity couldn't understand much of it, she heard as well.

"I'm out of here." Viv finally had all she could take. Blowing Wills a kiss, she added, "Happy birthday, Wills. Save me a slice of that yummy birthday cake." And she left.

GiGi, realizing both Mary and Viv had left the birthday celebration because of her, felt a sudden pang of guilt.

"Tate and Wills, your GiGi owes you an apology. I really am sorry for causing such a ruckus." The sudden remorse became tear filled and genuine. Taking her napkin, the saucy grandma dabbed her eyes. "I'm just so jittery lately from seeing this family so upside-down and topsy-turvy. I'm a person of peace, you know. I've never been able to deal with upheaval real well. If something happens to me and I die tonight, because, you know, I am getting older and could drop dead at any moment, I just want you children to know my heart was always in the right place. And I love all of you. I really do."

"Nothing is going to happen to you, GiGi. Of course we know your heart is in the right place," Wills immediately spoke up. "This whole thing is my fault, and I'm the one who is sorry."

In life, there are times when remaining silent is best; however, this was not one of those times. Wisdom finally poked Philip in the gut, urging him to say something.

"This isn't anyone's fault. We live in a fallen world full of darkness, and that old enemy, the devil, is prowling around right now, seeking to destroy this family. Hear me say this out loud...it ain't gonna happen! You can get behind us, Satan, because we belong to Jesus!"

"Yes, Lord," Poppy mumbled, eyes now closed, praying for Mary.

"I love this whole family so much." Philip started to cry. "It would be impossible to measure the depths of my love for each one of you." It took a few seconds for Philip to gather the composure to continue.

"And love is going to carry us through this, because love conquers all kinds of evil. Do you believe that?" Philip looked around the table, purposefully catching the eyes of Tate and Wills.

"I believe it, Daddy." Tate's voice was so soft and sweet.

"Me too," added her big brother's much deeper voice.

"Your momma and I are being tested. That's all this is. In fact, this whole family is being tested. And we are going to pass this test, and all future tests, with flying colors! Do you know why?" he asked.

"Because love conquers all," replied GiGi.

Philip reached across the table, taking his mother-in-law's hand in his.

"Exactly," he agreed.

Chapter 19

The preacher and his wife, Jeannie, were the ideal hosts. A match made in heaven, they not only shared the spiritual gift of serving others, but they equally exemplified the patience of Job. Those innate qualities made the charge of caring for a rambunctious teenage boy fairly easy. Crew had spent three nights with them with no incidents. So far, so good.

The idea of a parsonage is a distant memory for most towns and cities, but this particular reverend still occupied the quaint, white, clapboard home occupying a corner of the church's ten rolling farm-like acres. Paint willfully pried itself away from the wood on the country home, determined to reveal its age to all those who visited. Now more than seventy years old, the place had housed Preacher Walker when he was a young boy. Both of his parents, in fact, were buried in the church's cemetery. Oh, he felt proud to be a second-generation pastor of the Hopewell Baptist Church.

Each afternoon, the two soul mates, who were ever bound by routine, meandered their way over to the church building to spend a few hours serving the Lord by way of cleaning the building. To some church leaders, being relegated to janitor might present a pride issue, but to Preacher Walker and Jeannie, caring for the Lord's house was the same as caring for Jesus Himself. Often singing hymns of praise, they swept, mopped, and dusted the building, representing uncommon humility.

On Tuesdays, they tackled the church's kitchen...Wednesdays, the fellowship hall...Thursdays, the Sunday-school classrooms...Friday, the bathrooms...and Saturday was a day to prepare for their Sunday-morning service by doing what they referred to as "a good once-over," which amounted to a full day's work of tidying things up. The church building was used on Wednesday evenings for a potluck dinner, prayer meeting, and choir practice, but other than that, it was empty and quiet during the week. It was hard to believe their membership at one time had reached more than three hundred. But after the church pianist had left her husband for a deacon several years ago, the congregation had split. Now, they were fortunate if Sunday mornings brought two hundred people. It didn't bother them. With statistics showing a general decline in church attendance nationwide, the Walkers were pleased with the regular attendees they had somehow managed to keep.

While playing the role of custodians in the church, Preacher Walker and Jeannie often hearkened back to the days when the church was an extension of the family, to the time when parishioners visited the church nearly every day. Some would stop by for prayer, others to meet about planning future church activities. Whatever the reason, they came. The two, now married to one another for most of their lives, cherished their memories and loved reliving the past.

If they could put their finger on the one thing they discussed most often, it was VBS, Vacation Bible School. They longed to go back in time, if even if for a moment, to revisit the weeks of summer Bible school when families came from all over the city, joining together at Hopewell Baptist Church, to celebrate the Lord. Babbling children would line up single file all the way around the church building according to their grade in school, and then they marched in, filling the pews one at a time. After reciting the pledge to the American flag, the Christian flag, and the Bible, they were broken up to work on age-specific art projects, to hear Bible stories through the use of silly puppets, and to compete in physical activities and games, all geared to teach them about a God who not only created them but who also loved them.

Parents even joined in, teaching classes, cooking for the children, and simply enjoying fellowship together. The evenings would begin at six o'clock and would sometimes run until ten or later. To the preacher and Jeannie's best recollection, God always smiled on Bible school week, because for the life of them, they couldn't remember a single rainstorm ever interrupting the fun.

For the Walkers, those uncomplicated summer days represented the best days of their lives. The new technologically advanced world had, in their opinion, left the wonders of yesteryear behind in the dust. Communication was now accomplished by way of the Internet, and entertainment for youth now centered around gaming systems, cell phones, television, drugs, and sexual pleasure. If it broke their hearts that people no longer took the time for a face-to-face visit, they knew it must break the heart of the Savior. So day after day, they kept up their routine, opening their lives for a random visitor who might walk through the door.

Of all the days of the week, aside from Sunday (of course), Monday was their favorite; it was the day they spruced up the sanctuary, or the "War Room," as they jokingly called it. An eighteen-foot vaulted ceiling brandished hand-hewn wooden beams; the dark wood was punctuated by walls painted in the palest of blue. Six enormous stained-glass windows stood watch over the grand room, telling the story of Jesus and his twelve disciples through a mosaic picture; turquoise, red, and gold captured the sunlight, sending colors to playfully dance at their own whim throughout the space. Beneath one of the windows was a golden plaque bearing the name of a church member who had fallen from a ladder and died while working with the construction crew in that very room. The windows had been his widow's gift to the church, installed in his memory.

As for the floors, taupe carpeting provided a cozy cushion for feet, setting off the antique cherry pews meticulously placed in lines to leave one large center aisle. And behind the pulpit, above the baptistery, was yet another magnificent stained-glass window. Unlike the other six, which were long and rectangular, this one was a perfectly round circle. The colorful, odd-shaped pieces of glass were painstakingly put together to depict the Savior, not hanging on a cross, but raised from the dead, arms outstretched, bearing nail-scarred hands. This was a relatively new addition, a little more than two years old, and had been a gift from the Montgomery family in memory of Mary's grandfather, GiGi's father, and Preacher Walker's best friend. Preacher Walker had called him Mr. Ben, and every time the old pastor walked into the "War Room," he thought of his friend and dearly missed him.

Mary had attended the church her entire life. The building was as much home to her as her own home. She knew the pastor's schedule as well as he did, so on this Monday, following the horrid police raid at Crew's house, she timed her arrival perfectly.

"Mary, hon, what brings you by here?" Jeannie rose from her knees and welcomed her with open arms.

"Oh, I didn't mean to interrupt; I was hoping I could sneak in," she replied.

Preacher Walker pushed himself to standing and came alongside Jeannie. "As long as we've been at this church, I'm fairly certain we'd hear a li'l mouse if he were to change his routine. I think you're a little bit nosier than a li'l old mouse, don't you?" he laughed.

Mary loved the Walkers. They never ceased to make her feel at ease. "I know you all are busy praying over the pews, and I just wanted to join you today if that's all right." Mary asked the question knowing what their answer would be. This wouldn't be the first time she'd joined them.

Preacher Walker didn't even hesitate. "Well, you know our routine, so whatcha say we get to prayin'?"

The three knelt in the expanse of the sanctuary, each taking a separate pew. Going from bench to bench, they took turns praying out loud over those who had occupied the space the day before.

The five-member Johnson family typically sat in the third pew, on the right side of the lectern. They had an aging family member who was losing her memory to Alzheimer's disease and who now needed around-the-clock care. Preacher Walker prayed out loud: "Lord, Old Timer's Disease has gotten hold of Mrs. Beverly's mind. We love her, Father, and we know You love her even more than we do. Watch over her, and bring peace to her family this week."

Mary thought of the Dasher family when she came to the fifth pew on the left side of the lectern. The couple always arrived early on Sundays so they could be there to greet everyone. She paused and pictured them in her mind, seated in the pew with their arms around their daughter and with their granddaughter, Lexi, seated proudly up in her grandfather's lap.

"Father, would you bless and protect the Dasher family this week? And continue to be near little Lexi as she prepares to go through another surgery to correct her cleft palate. Thank you for sending them our way; they bring our church family such joy."

Jeannie came to pew number six on the right side. She thought of the widow who had been a member of their church for more than twenty years.

"Jesus, You know the needs of Judy better than I do. She must be missin' her best friend an awful lot; some days, she says she don't even get out of bed...can't bear life without him. Show us how we can meet her needs better, Lord. Hug her tight, and bring her comfort only You can bring."

Pew after pew, they knelt and prayed, all the time avoiding the first pew on the right side. After hitting every other bench and running out of church members to pray for, Preacher and Jeannie moved as one toward Mary's pew.

"C'mon, Mary. This is why you're here, ain't it?" The older man could read her like a book and didn't care to call her out. "Let's just sit right here for a minute; whatcha say?"

Preacher Walker and Jeannie sat down, leaving an open space between them for Mary to sit. When she plopped down, each took one of her hands, interlocking their fingers with hers. To them and to her, she instantly became Mary, the little girl, again. The one they'd known since she was an infant.

"Every time I look at that stained-glass window of Jesus, I think of your granddaddy, Mary." The pastor was just getting started, his eyes looking up at the colored glass.

"Me too." She squeezed their hands to let them know how much she appreciated them.

"What did you love most about him?" he asked.

She didn't rush to give an answer. The beauty of being with the preacher and Jeannie was that they were happy to take life at a slow pace, never in a hurry like the rest of the world seemed to be. Her mind took her back to times her grandfather called her to come in from the outside for lunch. She could still hear his voice. He'd take her hands in his and wash them with sweet-smelling soap, taking the time to make sure the water was always perfectly warm. "OK, baby, we've got to get these hands good and clean before you eat." Just like that, she could actually feel her hands in his.

Her reflections took her to the many times he'd tucked her into bed when she stayed overnight at his and Grandmomma's house...she closed her eyes and felt the cool, satiny sheets on her bare toes...the fuzzy, Windex-blue blanket he'd tucked around her...she even felt his smooth face against hers as he kissed her good night. He always smelled like aftershave.

Her next memory settled upon the very pew she was seated in. She could see her grandfather singing in the choir while her grandmother sat in a wheelchair at the end of the pew. He would look down from the choir loft, smiling at her and her grandmother. Mary may have been using her mind's eye, but the vision was so real that she could even hear her grandmomma singing the old hymn: "When We All Get to Heaven." She allowed herself to linger in it, knowing the preacher and Jeannie wouldn't mind.

Next she recalled her grandmother's hair and makeup. Why had she not thought about that before? Her hair was always carefully brushed and blush perfectly applied. What an amazing man her grandfather had been to take the time to minister to even the small details of her grandmother. Her thoughts then traveled to the close of each church service. She saw herself watch as her grandfather gently lifted her grandmother out of her wheelchair, placing her safely inside the car.

She broke away: "I loved the way he loved his family, especially my grandmomma."

A couple of minutes passed as the three reflected.

"I've been leadin' this church for a long time, Mary, and I've met some mighty men of God through the years, but I've never met anybody who compared to Mr. Ben and Mrs. Elaine. When I first met your granddad and grandmomma, I was taken aback by both of 'em. She required his constant care, twenty-four hours a day, and he gladly served her as if she were a queen. And, oh boy, did she love him." His voiced cracked as he spoke. "They taught me and Jeannie so much about what it really means to lay down your life for somebody."

The three continued to hold hands, looking straight on at the face of Jesus in the glass. Glimpses of sunlight filtered in. Mary shared her heart: "Do you know what I wonder? I wonder if God made me their granddaughter because He knew Miss Charity would be in my life someday. Do you know, every time I pull out Miss Charity's handicap stroller...when I feed her...when I dress her...when I lift her in and out of the car...I think of them."

"Mary, every time I see you caring for our little Miss, I think of 'em too." The irony had not been lost on the elder gentleman.

They fell silent again. Taking their time. Allowing the Spirit to lead. The church door opened. The door opened?

"Hey, Preacher! Are you here?" Crew called out. He'd been with the Walkers for three nights in a row, ever since the police raided his party, but he was now ready for some freedom. "Preacher!"

"We're in here, buddy!" the pastor shouted back.

Noticing Mary right away, Crew hesitated as he entered the sanctuary.

"Well, are ya gonna come in, or aren'tcha?" Preacher Walker turned around and shot him a teasing grin. "We've certainly got enough room for you in here...the place is empty."

Jeannie decided to speak up.

"Mary, I don't think you and Crew have had much time to catch up lately, have you?"

"No, we haven't." Mary stood to face the boy who, in her estimation, had caused most of her troubles of late. She nervously toyed with her hair, unsure how to respond. "How have you been, Crew?"

"I'm all right."

Surrounded by the church where she'd given her heart to Jesus, standing beside the man who had led her in the sinner's prayer, Mary became overwhelmed with a feeling of shame and sorrow. When had she allowed hatred for this boy to take root? And why had she allowed her hatred to come between herself and her family? As reality set in, Mary the Believer couldn't help it; she reached out to hug Crew.

"Are you really all right?"

His nerves got the best of him too. He was stiff and even pulled away a little bit, but she had known him for so many years...she didn't let go. His body finally relaxed. He let her hug him, and as they embraced, their hurt left them.

"Crew, I have been wrong. I was so afraid of you and Wills getting into trouble, I totally forgot my faith. That concussion and those crazy Lemon Drop Parties just about took me down."

Mary tugged the teenager's arm and invited him to sit on the first pew with her, the Montgomery family pew. Preacher Walker and Jeannie joined them, serving as bookends.

"I've got an idea, Crew. Every Monday, before Jeannie and I clean up this room, we come in here and pray over every pew. We pray particularly for the people who sit in 'em week after week." He patted the old, wooden bench. "This is the only one we've got left today, and since we've all already prayed, why don't you say the prayer for the Montgomery family?"

"I can't pray." Crew's expression was priceless. He'd been taken totally off guard.

"Can you talk?" the elder man asked.

"Yeah," Crew replied.

"Well, then you can pray. Prayin' just means you're talkin' to God. Have you ever talked to God about the Montgomery family?"

"No." He felt silly.

"After all these years, I think it's high time you do. Let's all kneel down at this pew and let Crew have his time to pray." Preacher Walker knelt down, motioning for everyone else to follow his lead.

"Take as much time as you need, son. We ain't in no hurry, and neither is God."

Crew joined them, kneeling. He looked around at each of them, noticing that everyone's head was bowed down and all eyes were closed. His heart pounded. He closed his eyes and bowed his head.

"God, thank You for the whole Montgomery family. They are the nicest people I've ever met—well, them and Preacher Walker and Mrs. Jeannie. I don't really know what else to say, so I guess I just want to say thank You. Oh, and if You don't mind, could You please heal my momma and Miss Charity? Amen."

"Amen," Mary agreed. She reached over, placing her hand on the boy's hand. "You've always been like one of our own. You're going through a tough time with your family, and we want to help...to be there for you however you need us. Just ask, OK?"

She meant it. Taking time to remember her grandparents and her Christian roots had softened her heart, and God had resumed control.

Crew wanted to trust her; he wanted to trust all of them. But the chains holding his heart were unyielding.

"I'm going back home today, but thanks anyway. Preacher and Mrs. Jeannie asked me to run by and let them know when I was leaving, so that's why I came barging in on you all. I'm really sorry about that. A friend is waiting on me outside since I didn't get to drive myself over here, so I better go." He flashed a confident smile, the one that portrayed a carefree teenager, the one that usually fooled everyone. But this time, no one in the room was fooled.

The preacher walked with him to the door. "You know, we went to a lot of trouble to keep you at our house the last few days, wouldn't you say?"

"Um, yes, and I am so sorry about that. Let me know if I can do anything to pay you back."

"I was sure hoping you'd say that. You see, I'm embarrassed to admit it, but I need your help on Sunday morning at our service. I've been told you're awfully good with electronics, and the guy who usually runs our sound system is gonna be out on Sunday. I need you to show up here at nine in the mornin' to get set up and to run our sound in the service."

The pastor didn't ask but gave an order. Crew didn't answer.

"Jeannie and I were good to you, weren't we? We fed you, gave you a warm home to sleep in, and your own bed..." He stopped to give Crew the opportunity to answer.

"All right. I'll be here. I'm not making any promises, but I'll try to help you out."

The two shook hands. Preacher Walker's trap had worked.

Mary walked up behind the old man of God, surprised by how crafty he had proven to be:

"You know, it sure is odd that Crew showed up here at the same time as me."

"It sure is, ain't it?" he replied, looking out the door, watching Crew and his friend pull away.

"Who called you?" Mary asked.

The pastor closed the door and spun around to face Mary. "Called me?" he asked with a bright smile.

"Was it GiGi or Poppy?"

"What in the world are you talkin' about?" he giggled slyly.

Jeannie joined them in the vestibule. "Who do you think called him, Mary?"

"That woman can't help but meddle, can she?" Mary rolled her eyes and gave a huff, thinking of how she'd asked her mom and dad to come stay with Tate and Miss Charity so she could go to the church.

"Easy, Mary. Today, I think God is on the meddler's side." The man with the gentle soul laughed out loud from the pit of his gut this time, considering all the times he knew GiGi had cooked up trouble with her two daughters.

"But here's the real funny part; and brace yourself, 'cause you really are gonna think this is hilarious. Your momma told me she is prepared to keep the kids for the rest of the day, just so you can stay here and help me and Jeannie clean the sanctuary...ain't that nice of her?"

Jeannie gave a snicker under her breath. "Go grab the vacuum cleaner, Mary, 'cause it looks like you're gonna be here awhile."

"Listen, I know when I've been had!" Mary exclaimed while going to the storage closet to help them pull out cleaning supplies. "I can hear her now: 'She can stay and help you clean today while I serve the Lord by caring for my grandchildren! Maybe being in God's house will do Mary some good.' I swear, that woman is a busybody."

"Mary, do you remember Vacation Bible School?" The preacher, holding a dustcloth and furniture polish, changed the subject.

Mary answered while dragging the vacuum cleaner into the large expanse, searching the walls for an outlet. "Of course I do; you know how much I loved VBS."

"Do you still remember the pledge you kids used to say to the Bible?" he asked, now spraying the seat of a pew with polish and rubbing it down.

"Yes, I do, because I am an exceptional student, remember? Am I going to need to prove it to you?" Mary turned, giving a wink at Jeannie, who was busy making sure each pew contained a welcome card and a pencil.

"As a matter of fact, you are...wait right there for half a second, and don't start the vacuumin' yet."

Mary watched the man wearing his dress pants, dress shoes, and button-down scuttle off to the small room behind the choir loft. She cracked up thinking about how he must be the only man on earth who would take the time to dress up to clean a building. Within an instant he returned, carrying a Bible.

"Come on down front, Mary," he said, now appearing to be on cloud nine. "This was my favorite part of Bible school. I loved hearing the children's voices, all together, making this pledge."

It dawned on her this wasn't a joke. He actually wanted her to recite the pledge to the Bible. As she walked down front, very slowly, she started saying the words in her head, hoping to locate them somewhere in the far recesses of her mind. It had been years since she'd said or heard the pledge to the Bible.

"I'm not sure I'll be able to remember this," she admitted, not wanting to disappoint them.

"You've heard the old sayin'...it's like ridin' a bike, Mary." He beamed, holding up the Bible, just as he had done every year in Bible school. His hair was now crowned with white, but his face had not changed much at all. The man with one of the most gentle souls on earth grinned ear to ear when she started.

"I pledge allegiance, to the Bible, God's Holy Word..."

They joined her: "I will make it a lamp unto my feet and a light unto my path and will hide its words in my heart that I might not sin against God."

Silence.

Peace.

Fond memories of old.

So many years had passed, but those words, said year after year...and the memories, still alive in that room...were common ground. Foundation. Tradition and faith held them together; their lives were eternally entwined.

"See, Mary? I told you it's like ridin' a bike," he beamed. "Praise the Lord! God's Word is hidden in your heart, girl. You proved that today. Just remember what I taught you when you were a wee thing. The Bible can be summed up in two statements. What are they?"

She answered: "The first one is to love God; the second is to love people."

"Oh, I am so proud of you. By lovin' Crew today, you lived out your pledge to the Bible. And I got to witness it." The pastor laid the Bible on the pulpit, treating it like a prized possession, and went back to dusting.

For the rest of the day, the three relived the good old days together as they cleaned. At times, their laughter echoed in the room, bouncing off the walls and all around. Life is funny, isn't it? The very best times are often those spontaneous moments that haven't been planned out at all.

If the three had had spiritual eyes, they would've seen a crowd of angels in the sanctuary pews that day as they prayed, vigilantly guarding each and every spoken word. They also would have heard the pledge to the Bible being recited, in unison, by them all. That day, on the edge of a small town in Tennessee, a mother, a pastor, and a pastor's wife entertained angels. And in heaven, Mr. Ben and Mrs. Elaine, Grandmomma and Granddaddy, were looking on, interceding in prayer on their behalf.

Life was getting better, but the battle was not over yet.

Chapter 20

A few months passed. Peace, as easy as a leaf carried by a gentle breeze, flittered about, finally choosing its resting place upon the Montgomery family. Mary and Philip made up. Their marriage was superb again. She had apologized, and Philip was quick to forgive. They agreed to reach out and offer support to Crew, who had responded to their kindness by joining them for dinner most every night. They had even given him a key to their home so he could come and go as he pleased, a true sign of trust on their part.

Crew now spent weekends with Preacher Walker and Jeannie, enjoying their attention and Jeannie's home-cooked meals. He worked with them at cleaning the church on Saturdays and was proud of his new job as the lead sound man during Sunday-morning service. It had taken time for the fair-haired teenager to lay his baggage down and open his heart to risk loving again, and though he still had a long way to go, he was on his way. All the partygoers who had been caught at the now-infamous "Lemon Drop Party Bust," including Wills and Crew, had completed their community-service work, painting the walls of a local elementary school in need of some fixing up. And Crew had kept his promise to not have any more parties. Marijuana was still a daily struggle for him, but as he embraced the chance of being a part of a "family," his use had been steadily dwindling.

As for Miss Charity, she had her heart check, and it was a good one. The echocardiogram showed some slight changes, but immediate repair would not be necessary. The Montgomery clan was given a reprieve and wouldn't have to go to the next heart check for six months. Precious harmony was not lost on Mary; she relished it every morning during her Bible-study time, thanking God for His goodness. At first, loving Crew had been a challenge for her; however, over time, as she allowed herself to open up, the Lord replaced her insecurities toward the boy with compassion for him. He was fast becoming an integral part of her family life.

No one asked Crew about his mother and father, which was odd considering the incredible circumstances. The town's rumor mill had effectively spread the news of his crazy momma and absentee father; word had even made the local *Bradley County Chitty Chat* gossip paper days after the Lemon Drop Party Bust. Maybe Cleveland was one of those small towns, the kind that talked about the oddity of a person's family life behind closed doors while doing nothing to get involved...or perhaps no one really cared aside from Philip, Mary, Preacher Walker, and Jeannie, who were too afraid to bring up the subject...whatever the reason, the town underestimated the Cutless family, especially Bonnie Cutless.

Crew's mom and dad had met in their twenties, set up on a blind date by a mutual friend. Carter

Cutless came from old money. Bonnie came from nothing but made up for what she lacked with breathtaking beauty. At five feet ten inches, she never allowed herself to weigh more than one hundred and thirty pounds. Straight, blond hair, always perfectly highlighted, reached down and kissed the middle of her back. What she was known most for, however, were crystal-blue eyes that captivated all who dared sneak a peek at them. She was forty but still looked twenty-five...thirty at most. She was five years younger than Carter, and all who knew her said she'd married him for his money. They were correct.

When Bonnie was a little girl, her mother prostituted her body to put food on the table, but mostly to feed an addiction to alcohol. She and her mother lived in a trailer park for several years, surviving on very little, until the day a man calling himself a deacon knocked on their door offering hope of Jesus and a better life. That evening, he moved them out of their trailer and into a communal-type home, where everyone was "married" to the head pastor and where alcohol and drugs were in abundance. Bonnie was homeschooled by the women of the commune along with the other children, but as she blossomed, many of the women became jealous of her. At thirteen years of age, she was pushed out and into the foster-care system. She never saw her mother again.

Feelings of despair overwhelmed Bonnie at first. The adjustment to life outside of the cult was a big one. And even though her mother hadn't been a good one, she missed her. As Bonnie was shuffled about in the system, her despair turned to bitterness...and eventually hatred. She had watched the women in the commune unabashedly throwing themselves at the pastor and the deacons to gain favors, and she had been a good student. As she went from foster home to foster home and from school to school in the greater Atlanta area, she sought out the boys and men who had wealth and allowed them to have their way with her...for a price. By the time the opportunity with Carter Cutless came along, she was a pro. He was snagged and being dragged down the aisle before he realized she'd even baited her hook.

For a few years, Carter and Bonnie were happy, as most young married couples are. Her exceeding beauty garnered Carter a lot of attention with his coworkers and peers. But it didn't take long for him to tire of her manipulative tactics and strange behavior. And when she read the signs that their relationship was waning, Bonnie quickly became pregnant with Crew to make sure she kept her grip on his money.

Carter, in his own mind, was a big-time successful banker. It was true he was invited to nearly every charity event and societal occasion known to man in the southeastern part of the United States, often making the headlines at the events he chose to attend, but the truth was, his popularity had nothing to do with work and everything to do with a tremendously large portfolio loaded with blue chips left to him by his maternal grandparents. As favor for him grew with the general public, he found less mercy for Bonnie. He hadn't a clue (or a care) about her past, so putting two and two together in an effort to "fix things" was never an option. Over time, they grew more and more distant from one another; and by the time they moved to Cleveland, Tennessee, their marriage was in name only. He worked around the clock, renting a two-bedroom apartment in Chattanooga near his office while she kept things spotless at their home, a good forty-five minutes away from him. An obsessive-compulsive nature imprisoned her every waking minute except for the times she was running back and forth to the Cleveland Country Club. Golf had become her favorite hobby and her fixation, and until recently, she had been one of the wealthiest club members.

Crew had never been close to either of his parents. He'd always felt like more of a "thing" to be cared for, more like a pet than a human being. His father, hungry for power, gorged himself with more and more money and notoriety. That kind of lifestyle choice left no time for dealing with a son, though he made an obligatory call or text to Crew nearly every day to check in. Bonnie, in contrast, resented everything about Crew. Fury burned inside her at the mere thought of him. Her mother had kicked her to the curb, so she had the full intention of allowing her son to feel the exact same pain she'd felt. Locking him out of the main house, forcing him to live alone in the basement, was retribution on her part. Her mother had done it to her, and she was passing along the torch.

For all Crew knew, his mother didn't keep up with a single detail about his life. He honestly felt she birthed him just so she could torture him with neglect. Other than the two or three football games his parents attended together each year for show, along with an occasional family get-together with Carter's family in Georgia, he didn't see her or talk to her. But Crew was wrong. His mother's OCD ran much deeper than keeping her body in perfect shape, scrubbing her house from top to bottom on a daily basis, and popping a pill every four to five hours. Her biggest addiction was him.

Bonnie sat in her bedroom, on the king-sized Louis Philippe Sleigh bed, facing a custom-made, full-length mirror that took up half the wall. As she brushed her hair, she spoke to the reflection looking back at her:

"Mary, you think you are going to steal my son away from me, don't you?"

It was four minutes past two o'clock in the afternoon; Bonnie had just showered after her workout and was stroking her hair with the paddle brush one hundred times. She didn't know why one hundred was a magic number, but she had done it for as long as she could remember. Her brush pulled at her long, blond hair for the sixty-fourth time.

"That is a big mistake, and it is going to cost you dearly." She stopped and threw the brush into the mirror with all her might, causing the glass to splinter into tiny cracks in the area where the brush hit.

She'd stopped brushing on number...oh, God, she couldn't recall what number she was on when she stopped brushing. She began again with number one. Buffing her nails would be next in her personal-hygiene ritual, followed by tweezing her brows, a pedicure, and then meticulously applying makeup.

After reaching the number one hundred, Bonnie picked up the phone and quickly dialed a local business to set up an appointment for them to come replace the mirror. The nagging feeling of needing to get that mirror repaired was driving her nuts.

"No, I need someone to come out tomorrow. Period. I cannot wait until next week."

After she gave the salesman exact measurements and offered to pay a significant amount of extra money for his readjusting his schedule to accommodate her, the salesman agreed to make a trip to Bonnie's house the next morning. Satisfied, she then pulled a tissue from the tissue box on the bedside table and cleaned the phone while checking the time.

At two thirty, Bonnie was seated in her bathroom floor filing and buffing her nails. Each step in her hygienic routine had to begin on the quarter hour, half hour, or hour. The overly obsessive blonde kept a close watch on the clock to keep it that way, because she secretly believed her beauty would fade if she didn't.

"The broken mirror might bring bad luck," she said. "I'll have to keep every piece of the glass, bathe in some salt water, and burn incense. That should take care of it."

She wondered how she would sleep that night for worrying about it. The dread of bad luck became her tormentor, and by nightfall, she knew she would have to numb the thoughts with a bit of extra poison. She continued her discussion with herself.

"Mary, Mary, quite contrary, how does your family grow? By stealing boys from other moms...oh, Mary, this game is gonna blow!"

Chapter 21

"Whenever someone comes to me expressing a concern that she might be suffering from some sort of mental illness, her expression of that concern is the first clue telling me she is not," a wise doctor once told Mary when she was battling some depression following Miss Charity's first open-heart surgery.

"But sometimes I have crazy thoughts; there have been times when I've even believed I am living in an alternate reality," she had told him, to which he replied: "You are here, telling me about those thoughts, Mary, which means you are very aware of them. If you were unaware that those thoughts were unusual, and if you were acting upon them, then we'd have reason for alarm."

The same could not be said for Bonnie Cutless. In her mixed-up world, she was the only sane person, and everyone else was to blame for all of her troubles. She rummaged through her son's belongings every day after he left for school and justified her actions by blaming him for being untrustworthy. When she found the Montgomery family's house key hidden in the toe of one of Crew's athletic socks, she blamed Philip for being so stupid as to give her son a key to his home. And when she had a copy of the key made for herself, she placed full responsibility on Mary for trying to take her son away from her. Bonnie didn't have any problems; everyone else had plenty of them.

Absorbed in a life rhythm ordered by strict routine, it didn't take Bonnie long to figure out Mary Montgomery's weekly schedule, if you could call it a schedule. Bonnie couldn't imagine how anyone could live a life so lax and unpredictable. She resented Mary for it, because to her, it amounted to laziness at best and negligence at worst. But within a few months, she had become versed in most every detail of Mary's life, discovering her closest friends, her favorite foods, and even the makeup she wore. She kept every detail listed in a steno pad hidden beneath her mattress. Mary, always busy either tending to Miss Charity's constant needs or rushing to run errands whenever time allowed, never noticed she was being followed. Outside the display of utter chaos, Bonnie's nemesis did have one constant routine. Like clockwork, Mary, Tate, and Miss Charity met Philip for breakfast at the Cracker Barrel on Monday mornings before doing their weekly grocery run, leaving the Montgomery home empty for a minimum of two hours.

The first time she broke into their home, Bonnie took time to investigate each and every room. She looked at photos displayed around the house, rooted through closets and drawers, and checked out the kitchen's pantry. She had never burglarized a home before, but because she was so convinced retribution was a necessity, Bonnie wasn't the least bit nervous about the crime. She was surprised to find she felt quite at home. Trudy wasn't sure about her at first; she sniffed the stranger's ankles and gave her a bark or two. But Miss OCD, who had covered every detail, came prepared with Trudy's favorite goody: Beggin' Strips. Poor Trudy sold out for a treat and was thereafter Bonnie's little buddy.

On her next plunder, she became gutsier, taking one item from every family member's bedroom. She swiped a Tennessee Volunteer T-shirt from Wills's dresser drawer, a purple hairbrush from the big wicker basket sitting on Tate's floor, a princess crown from the end of Miss Charity's bed, and a worn Bible from Mary's bedside table. An onlooker would've witnessed Bonnie casually passing from room to room, as comfortable as if the house were her own. She didn't take much thought about what she stole that day. For her, the act of stealing was more about the exercise of control.

After carefully placing the items in her car, which she had boldly parked in the driveway, Bonnie stowed them in a clear plastic tub in her closet. She marked "REVENGE" on the lid of the tub in big, bold letters alongside a big smiley face she had drawn with a permanent marker. Feeling exhilarated from playing her game, Bonnie had some extra pep in her step. The thought of getting caught never entered her mind.

"Have you seen Miss Charity's princess crown, Momma?" Tate asked that same night. "It's time for her bedtime story, and I can't tell her a story without her crown."

Mary answered while helping Tate look around the house: "You're right! The little princess will not be happy at all if she has to listen to a princess story without her crown!"

They searched high and low to no avail, even employing Philip and Wills to help.

"I'm telling you, Momma, I'm pretty sure I put it on her bed this morning after I helped her make it up. That's what I always do, you know?" Tate added when they all decided to give up the quest.

"Stay right here, and don't move a muscle! I've got an idea!" Mary dashed out of the room and into her bedroom, returning within a few minutes with her hands tucked behind her back. She proceeded to speak with a heavy British accent: "Wills, go fetch our little princess, please, sir." She gave her son a nod with a grin plastered across her face.

"I guess I'm at your service, Queen Mother." Wills bowed while speaking with his own version of a goofy British accent. He then retreated to find the princess. In no time at all, he came marching back into the room, pretending to be a high-ranking solider, with the little miss tucked beneath his arm, swinging her legs all around in an effort to be released from his grip.

"Here she is, Madame!" He placed the little one gently on the ottoman in front of the sofa. "Do with her as you must, but please be gentle." Wills backed away, head down.

Mary played along. "Oh, thank you, kind soldier. You will be rewarded greatly for your service. In fact, please, go now...to the pantry...and fetch yourself a Little Debbie. Make it two."

Racing to the pantry, Wills didn't give his mother time to change her mind. "Oh, you are far too kind, my queen!"

Mary continued: "Now, as for you, little princess. It seems a wonderful thing has happened today. The crown you once wore was for a baby princess, but as of today, you have become a big-girl princess. And to celebrate this day, you will now be wearing a very special big-girl princess crown."

Mary bowed her head, gave a curtsy, and pulled a beautiful, sparkling tiara from behind her back, holding it out in both her hands, as if it were extremely valuable, so that Tate and Miss Charity could get a good look. Tate couldn't contain herself.

"Oh, Momma...I mean, Queen Mother...that is a real-life crown!" She did her best to imitate the British accent.

"It certainly is. What do you expect for a real, big-girl princess?"

Tate crept up to her mother, not taking her eyes from the tiara. "May I?"

Mary, still maintaining her own very British accent, responded: "Of course you may."

Tate took the crown from her mother's hands and placed it carefully on Miss Charity's head. She was already dressed in her bright-pink footed pajamas.

"She looks beautiful, doesn't she?" Tate asked, admiring her little sister.

"Like a real princess," replied Philip, watching as Tate led her sister to her bedroom by the hand. Miss Charity gently touched the crown on her head and grinned as they walked.

Philip turned to Mary. "Where did you get that crown?"

"Long story," she answered.

Philip walked over to the kitchen to join Wills. "I've got time for a story; do you, son?"

Wills couldn't give up the accent: "Oh, my lady, I always have time for your stories." He popped the last bite of a Fudge Round into his mouth and smiled, chocolate goo coating his front teeth.

"Ganging up on the Queen Mother, are you?" she teased, joining them. "If you must know, the Queen Mother has dabbled in a few beauty pageants in her day. Of course, King Philip, you'll recall how I was first runner-up in all three of the Miss Cleveland pageants, to the utter dismay and embarrassment of our kingdom."

"Oh, dear, how have you ever lived it down?" asked Philip, teasing.

"Why, I'll be gobsmacked, Queen Mother! How do you show your face in this town?" Wills shouted with much drama, pretending to wipe a tear from his eye.

Mary folded her arms, giving them both a smirk with a roll of her eyes.

"Well, at some point along the way in my quest to win a beauty pageant, I was given that crown as a cheeky sort of consolation prize...and it has haunted me all these years...reminding me that I am simply a...well, a loser." She pretended to bite the back of her rolled-up fist, shooting them a look filled with agony. "I am so glad to finally pass it on to someone much more deserving than me."

"I still cannot believe I married a first runner-up, Wills. Why, oh why did I not go after one of those Miss Cleveland winners who have a real crown? One they actually earned?"

That was the last straw. Mary reached into a drawer, pulled out a plastic spatula, and came after Philip, pounding his rear end with it every step of the way, as they ran from room to room laughing.

Philip was the first to scream out: "You don't deserve me; you are but a first runner-up!"

Mary retorted, just as loud: "I will beat you with this spatula...into complete submission...until you recant every word, my lord!"

"I won't do it! I will never back down to a first runner-up!"

"You will!"

"I won't!"

Mary and Philip turned into high-school sweethearts all over again, giggling and teasing one another. Wills stood by enjoying every minute, reveling in the fact that his parents still loved each other after so many years. He chuckled to himself as he moseyed down the hall, peeking into Miss Charity's room to see the little princess listening intently as Tatum told her a story. The sparkling tiara still sat upon her head. He then leaned back against the bedroom door and smiled; everything in his life felt right.

Chapter 22

When Mary awoke early Tuesday morning, she couldn't find her Bible. It wasn't on the nightstand, and it wasn't in the front room where she did her Bible study every morning. She searched for the book everywhere in the house; she'd nearly turned the house upside down. Philip was still sleeping soundly, and though she hated to wake him, she gave his shoulder a few quick taps.

"Chief, I'm sorry, but can you wake up for just a minute?"

He was still in that morning fog, the kind of fog that causes you to question whether you are still in the middle of a dream, but he rounded up a half-mumbled answer: "Yeah, sure, what's wrong?" His eyes looked like unopened slits beneath his thick brows.

"I can't find my Bible. Have you seen it?"

Signaling that he would like to return to his snooze-fest, he rolled over in the bed, away from her. "No, I haven't seen it, but don't worry; I'm sure it will turn up somewhere."

"Yeah, little Miss probably took it and hid it somewhere. I'll find it." Mary left him to continue her search.

That missing Bible was one of her most prized possessions. A black, hardcover King James Version, it had a golden sword on the lower front right corner displaying the words: "Let the Word of Christ Dwell in You Richly." Through the years, Mary had used it for that purpose. Given to Mary by the church on the day of her baptism, the Bible was splattered with notes and different colors of highlights. It never left her house. She was so protective of it, as a matter of fact, that she took a different Bible with her to church on Sundays.

The remainder of that week, Mary spent time every day looking for her lost Bible. She didn't find the cherished book, and it never dawned on her that two prized items had gone missing within hours of one another. Mary, ever trusting and naive, kept believing the princess crown and the Bible would show up sooner or later.

Early spring had ushered in gleaming sunshine tempered by brisk temperatures guilty of trying to hang on too tightly to winter. Sunday morning looked and felt like a promising day to all those who welcomed it. Even the daffodil reared her buttery head notably throughout town, sprinkling the newborn grass with flowers endeavoring to imitate morsels of fresh, puffy popcorn that had magically been sprinkled on the ground overnight. The trees, not to be outdone, cut loose their annual grandiose show, busily clothing themselves with protective coats of apple, forest, and hunter green.

Stacking bulletins on the tables in the front entrance, Jeannie hummed a tune, looking forward to seeing her family, the church's members, walk through the door. Her short hair, once jet-black, was now punctuated by scads of gray. Silver-rimmed glasses hung precariously on the tip of her nose as she carefully double-checked the bulletin, making sure they were ready for each part of the prepared Sunday service. She patted her black patent flats on the floor to the rhythm of the tune as she hummed and read, freely allowing her long skirt to breeze back and forth against her stocking-covered calves.

Preacher Walker stood onstage testing the microphone, while Crew sat in the very back of the room adjusting the sound when Bonnie walked in.

"Hey, baby! I thought I'd find you here!"

She threw her hand up in Crew's direction, seemingly unaware of her all-too-casual greeting. The pastor swallowed hard, absentmindedly digging his toes deep into the ends of his shoes, planting his feet to make sure he didn't tip over from sheer shock. Crew stood from his chair, also completely blown away.

"Preacher Walker, isn't it?" Her long, silky, blond hair swished from side to side as she made her way up the aisle to the podium. A tight black dress, two inches above her knees, enveloped her body, hugging her thin frame. The old pastor didn't move. Couldn't move. At some point Jeannie stepped in from the back of the sanctuary, giving her husband a helpful nudge.

"Honey, have you met Bonnie Cutless, Crew's momma, yet?" She followed Bonnie to the front, saying a prayer in her heart: *Lord, please help him speak.* But Preacher Walker, thoroughly addled, couldn't find words.

She reached him and held out her hand. His gut reaction was to reciprocate, so he lifted his hand, and they shook. She didn't let go.

"I wanted to thank you, Pastor, for stepping in and taking care of Crew for me these past several weekends. I don't know if you are aware, but I've been having some health issues, so you and your wife have been a tremendous help to me." She looked him square in the eyes and lied with the utmost sincerity.

Crew was still standing in the back, heart thumping. She'd called him "baby" when she walked in, hadn't she?

The preacher finally said something.

"I'm so sorry; no, Jeannie and I sure didn't know you had been sick, or we would've come and visited you, or brought you some food or somethin'. We've been so happy to have Crew here to help us 'round the church on Saturdays and Sundays. He's our official sound man now." His voice shook, unmasking his trepidation for all in the room to see. He turned toward his wife. "Did you formally meet my wife…Jeannie?"

Bonnie still held his hand firmly in hers.

"We met as I was walking in. She was humming a tune and didn't see me at first. I must have stood there five minutes." She looked in Jeannie's direction. "What was that song? It was familiar to me."

She'd been standing there watching her humming a tune for five minutes? How had she missed her? Jeannie could think of nothing else. "Umm, I don't rightly know. I mean, I can't remember. I was just busying myself." She felt foolish.

Flashing her eyes back at the pastor, Bonnie intentionally gave his hand a solid squeeze before letting it go. She already had the preacher and his wife bamboozled, eating from the palm of her hand, but she silently wished they were both licking the bottoms of her black pumps. Like mangy animals. Thanks to her early experience with the cult, she could see right through all the religious hype and was determined to run the show.

Stepping away, she took a seat, knowingly, on the end of the Montgomery family pew. "So, what time does church start?"

"Everyone will start arriving any minute," Jeannie answered, trying her level best to appear upbeat and friendly. "I'm gonna need to go back in the foyer and hand out bulletins, so I hope you'll excuse me."

"Of course. Don't mind me. We'll talk some more after the service if that's OK with you. I'd really like to catch up." The blonde was unquestionably full of herself.

Catch up? Jeannie thought. *You've never given me the time of day.* But she didn't share her thoughts; instead she blurted out: "You know, Crew is havin' lunch over at our house after the service. You're welcome to join us." She then scooted away very fast, making a clean escape before Bonnie could give an answer. Preacher Walker followed her. So did Crew. And as soon as they were safely out of sight, the teenage boy grabbed the pastor's arms in a panic and started to speak just before Preacher Walker stopped him by raising his finger to his mouth.

"Shhhh. Don't say anything right now, all right? I wouldn't want your momma to hear us out here and think we're talkin' about her."

"But what is she doing here?" Crew saw it with his own two eyes but couldn't believe it.

The pastor again whispered: "I don't know, but she liked to have scared me half to death when she walked in the sanctuary. She is an intimidatin' somebody, ain't she?"

That brought a smile to Crew's face. "Tell me about it," he said.

Within minutes, families were drifting in, taking their pews. Preacher Walker and Jeannie greeted each person while Crew took his place back behind the soundboard, playing praise and worship music softly through the system. His mother never looked back in his direction. She sat like a statue, unmoving, facing forward.

Philip and Mary pulled into the parking lot right behind GiGi and Poppy. Poppy rushed over to their car once they parked, unbuckling the little Miss from her car seat and piling her along with her froufrou dress up in his arms. They all walked in together and were greeted by Jeannie, who filled them in on the special guest who was seated on their pew.

GiGi was aghast. "Well, I, for one, am not sitting next to that horrible excuse for a mother. Once we start singing hymns, and the Spirit fills this holy place, the good Lord may send a strike of lightning to zap her...and if that happens—and for the record, I wouldn't lose any sleep if it did happen—I don't want to be anywhere near her!"

"Calm down, Mom," Mary spoke under her breath. "Do you want people to hear you talking like that?"

"That's right," added Poppy, "if this is awkward for anyone, it's Crew. We need to act as normal as we can for his sake."

"I'll do it for Crew, but I'm warning you all." GiGi looked around at each of them, finger wagging. "I will pull out my Church of God roots and start speaking in tongues if I feel any demonic vibes escaping from that nutty woman."

"I think I may go sit with Crew today, if that's all right with everybody," interrupted Wills. Everyone nodded in agreement, and he rushed to console his best friend while the rest contemplated on how to best handle the situation.

"Now, GiGi, you have to behave yourself today." Poppy pulled his unpredictable wife up to the door so they could take a peek inside.

"There she is! Just look at her. Evil is hanging all around that woman in our pew...in *our* pew!" blurted out GiGi.

"Shhhh," Mary reminded her forcefully. "Don't start anything, Momma!"

Her mother purposefully let her purse roll off her arm and into her hand. She rotated around and batted the big Coach bag back at Mary with a huff, thumping her daughter's arm.

"What do you keep in that bag, Momma, a brick? Good grief; that really hurt!"

"No, that's not a brick you felt. I'm packing heat; that's what you felt. Maybe next time you won't be so quick to shush me!"

"Poppy, you let her bring her gun to church?" asked Mary, clearly not happy.

"Lord, Mary, do you think I'm stupid? We all knew once your momma got her license to carry, she'd be parading a fancy gun around, but not at the Lord's house. I drew the line there. The 'heat' she's carrying today is a big can of Raid Wasp Spray."

"And I'm not afraid to use it if I have to," added GiGi, nodding her head.

"Daaaaad...! You let her bring a can of wasp spray to church?" Mary exclaimed, her voice raised up at least an octave.

"She won't even stomp on a bug for fearin' she might break up its family...honey, you've got to believe me; your momma's just a big showboat. She saw on the social media that wasp spray works better than pepper spray, and she's been carrying it around with her ever since. She thinks it's the new big thing."

"Showboat my eye! This *is* the new big thing! A can of this juice will shoot poisonous spray twenty feet or more and blind a man." She gave her purse a big slap with her hand. "So if some yellow-bellied thief ever comes in this building thinking he can rob me or anyone else of their jewelry, he'll think twice when I start shaking my can around and spraying it straight into his eyes in the name of Jesus. There's no need to try and hide it. We live in a crazy world where a person's not even safe in the Lord's house anymore."

"A thief is never going to come into this church to rob the church people, so pipe down, Granny

Rambo." Poppy took his wife by the arm, still holding Miss Charity in his other arm. "Now come on in with me, and choose all of your words...and all of your actions...very wisely." GiGi, pouting, sauntered through the door and into the sanctuary, her arm in Poppy's. "And don't mention that spray can anymore, 'cause you make Mary nervous when you start talking like that," he instructed as they made their way down the center aisle.

GiGi didn't try to speak softly when she got the last word in: "That's my plan, Pops; gotta always keep everybody on their toes." She then gave her purse a final loud slap with her hand. "I may be a grandma, but nobody better mess with me." And with her last comment, she dropped her arm from her husband's and took the lead, marching down the aisle in one of her finest Sunday suits and high heels.

Poppy, looking smug, gave a laugh: "Little Miss, let's hope you never grow up to be as feisty as your GiGi."

Mary, Philip, and Tate followed closely behind them, dreading the impending meeting with Bonnie. Philip took a second to glance back at Crew, who was now catching up with Wills, and gave him a thumbs-up.

GiGi, naturally, was the first to arrive at the front pew. "Well, hello there...it is Bonnie, isn't it?" asked GiGi. "All these years, your son and Wills have been great friends; isn't it odd that we've never had a single conversation?"

"And I feel terrible about it, GiGi. Would it be OK with you if I call you GiGi?" Bonnie replied, reaching out her hand with all the appearances of a friendly handshake.

But GiGi wasn't about to give the demon vibes a chance to get hold of her, so she didn't reciprocate. "I've had a cold, honey, and don't want to make you sick. I think I'll just keep my hand to myself today." She made her way down the pew and sat down with a hard thump. Poppy, Miss Charity, and Tate joined her.

It was Mary's turn: "Good morning, Bonnie, I'm so happy to see you! It's been a while, hasn't it?"

"It certainly has. Much too long, Mary. And Philip, don't you look as handsome as ever?" Bonnie reached out her arms and gave Philip a big hug. Philip allowed his hands to touch her back in a stiff sort of way. She pulled back, leaving him with a peck on his cheek before repositioning herself back on the pew. Mary and Philip made their way past her, joining the others.

GiGi leaned over toward her daughter. "Did that demon woman just kiss your husband?"

"Mother, really?" Mary hoped her mother wouldn't mortify the family in front of the church body.

Poppy followed up by giving his wife the universal sign to zip her lip, but of course, she didn't listen. "If she lays her hands or her lips on Philip one more time, I'm taking her down like David took down that giant. I'll pull out every bleached-blond hair and stuff each one of 'em up her nose job before pounding the Botox clear out of her face...and I don't need a slingshot to do it...I'll take her down with my bare hands!"

Bonnie couldn't hear what was being said, but she knew they were talking about her. And she was pleased as punch about it.

The service had already begun when Viv entered, late as usual. No one, unfortunately, had the chance to warn her about the surprise visitor. As she walked down the center aisle toward the Montgomery family pew, she took notice of the long, blond hair and tried to place it. Preacher Walker was just beginning his sermon when she reached the pew and realized who it was. She attempted to pass over Bonnie, but Bonnie scooted over, making plenty of room for her at the end of the pew.

"Hey, Viv, honey." She patted the seat. "Just sit yourself right here next to me."

Viv sat still, going through the motions, pretending to listen to Preacher Walker's message, but in actuality, she was wholly preoccupied by the woman seated to her right. What on earth was she doing there?

GiGi elbowed Poppy in the ribs. "Oh, Lord, look...that demon woman has Viv trapped like a rat."

Poppy leaned over to ask his wife to please stop making comments, but in doing so, he inadvertently took his focus off of the little one seated in his lap. Miss Charity, who had already noticed her Aunt Viv down at the end of the pew, took that brief opportunity to hop off of his lap and make a dash toward Viv. Before anyone realized what had happened, Viv was snuggling her little niece close and kissing her on the softest part of her fuzzy neck. "How did you manage to get away from your Poppy and find your way down here to me?"

The little Miss gave a giggle out loud, fully realizing she had outwitted her grandfather.

"Poppy, what in the world are you doing? Look! You've let our little angel run down there with Viv, right next to the seed of Satan. God, we have to do something." GiGi whispered loud enough for Bonnie to hear this time.

In response, the blond bombshell leaned forward, returning the very loud whisper: "GiGi, dear, is there a problem? Should I move?"

GiGi, attempting to conceal that "crap, I've been caught" look, decided to make an attempt at her infamous ventriloquist impersonation, whispering without moving her lips: "Pops, pray for me, 'cause it looks like the demon woman knows I'm on to her."

She then opened her mouth very wide to silently mouth the next words to Bonnie. Pointing to her ear she mouthed, "I can't hear you." Then, pointing to the pastor, she added, "I'm trying to listen to the preacher." Leaning back in the pew, she again took up her ventriloquist act. "Don't worry, Pops; I think I took care of it."

Poppy, used to his wife's many antics, pretended to be so engrossed in Preacher Walker's sermon that he didn't hear or see anything going on around him.

Mary, however, didn't pretend not to see. Taking matters into her own hands, hoping to settle things quickly and politely, she scooted down to sit right next to Bonnie. "My mom is very protective over Miss Charity; that's all." She reached her arm around Bonnie's back and gave her a gentle squeeze. Placing her mouth close to her ear, she extended the gift of friendship: "We are all thrilled you are here."

Bonnie, in turn, leaned forward and looked over toward GiGi, who eventually felt the stare bearing into her. When their eyes finally met, the blonde gave the elder woman a big smile and a flitter of a wave before reaching over to Viv and pulling Miss Charity into her own lap. The message was clear to GiGi. Crew's mother was indeed a demon from the pit of hell.

Meanwhile, in the back of the room, Crew and Wills were engrossed in the scene. Crew's heart had not stopped racing since his mom's surprise entrance.

"Wills, what is my crazy mom up to?"

"I don't know, but my mom just hugged her, and now your mom is holding my little sister."

Crew shrugged his shoulders in dismay. Was hell freezing over, or what?

Chapter 23

Sunday night, Bonnie finished checking off the majority of her tasks and sat down with a glass of wine to journal about her day. It was official. For now, church would become a regular part of her weekly routine. Keeping her enemies a bit off-kilter, she would arrive at nine o'clock each Sunday, even though the service didn't begin until nine thirty.

"What kind of boneheaded pastor would begin an hour-long church service on the half hour?" she wondered. The thought wouldn't leave her: "Don't most events, no matter how big or small, begin *on* the hour?"

Bonnie's brain, now set on repeat, wouldn't let it go.

"How can I force this time issue without uncovering that I'm the one wanting to change things? Should I send an anonymous letter? I wonder if they would respond quicker to a suggestion or a threat. What if I left a random note somewhere in the church...maybe in the restroom, taped to a mirror...but which one? The men's or ladies' room? Or better yet, what if I left a note on the church's front doors? I could go old school and cut out letters from magazines and then glue them to a big poster board: 'God says to start your service at 9:00 a.m.!'" She laughed, considering how it would freak everyone out and possibly make the local news. "No one could trace something like that, could they? Wait. Is there camera surveillance that might catch me? No, I never saw a camera. That little redneck country church can't afford camera surveillance. Get a grip, Bonnie!"

She clenched her fists tightly. These kinds of thoughts were like open blisters to her, raw and fixed on plaguing every minute until she dealt with them. Lucky for her, though, she'd learned how to bandage her mind's maniacal rumination. Without hesitation, she abruptly shoved the fingernail of her right index finger deep underneath her left thumbnail until she felt the desired dose of pain without drawing blood. She stopped. Then she did it again. And stopped. Then she did it again. And again. And again. Until she had completed the ceremonial cleansing action one hundred times. No more. No less. She counted each, allowing the unrelenting discomfort to trump her obsessive thoughts about the church service time. Slight bruising would be the only sign left to show she'd wrestled with her thoughts, a small price to pay.

After finding mental relief, she finally wrote in her journal:

> *Went to church. Scared the hell out of Crew. He's a coward like his father. Worse than a coward. A wuss. The preacher and his wife are what I expected. Pathetic and weak.*

Selling Jesus and heaven as if they both exist. Liars. Then taking an offering at church. Surprise! Probably using the money to go on a cruise. Lowlife thieves. Spoke to Mary's mom for the first time. Psycho Lunatic. She has a problem with me. Stares a lot. I'd like to stomp her face. Sat in "Mary the Fool's" pew. She thinks I'm trying to be her friend. Philip noticed me today. Of course Philip noticed me. I kissed him in front of Mary. I think I'll seduce him. That will ruin Mary. The Down syndrome girl sat in my lap. It made everyone nervous. Jerks. I'd never hurt a disabled kid. She's the only decent one. I wish a Mack truck would fall from the sky and smash the rest of them. I'm going to church every Sunday now. As long as it suits. Was invited to the preacher's house for lunch. Didn't go. Think I'll go next week. Tomorrow I go to Mary's house again. Sunday I do church with Mary. Monday I

*steal from Mary. Jesus's
mother's name was Mary.
Stupid Cult.*

Crew, at the same time as his mother was cataloging her day, was in the basement getting ready to turn in for the night. He crept up the steps and reached to check the door. It had been months since he'd tested it, but after the bizarre day at church, curiosity wouldn't allow him to deny himself any longer. He gripped the handle and turned it slowly. It was locked. Responding to the familiar sting of hurt, he walked back down the stairs and lit up, taking only a couple of drags from his drug of choice. The pain left him. For the first time that day, his heart settled to a slow, steady beat. He recalled the text his dad had sent earlier in the day:

"Just checking in with you. Hope you have a great day, son!"

Crew decided not to return the message. His last thought for the evening was that neither of his parents would ever love him.

Upstairs, Bonnie washed down the prescription meds that lulled her off to sleep each evening with the final drops of red wine. She pulled down her bedding with five-star hotel precision and turned the light off, and then back on again, and then off, and then back on, and then off. Three times. Only one more item remained on the day's list. As she lay on her back, very much in the style of a mummy, she took a deep breath, embracing the tingling sensation that faithfully came each time she placed her body under her own authority. First she bent down all the toes on her right foot and then pulled them back. Next, she bent down all the toes on her left foot and pulled them back. Back and forth she bent them, back and forth and back and forth. "One Mississippi, Two Mississippi, Three Mississippi..."she said aloud in a rhythmic cadence, her toes brushing the top sheet as she moved them, creating a soft swishing noise. She looked forward to the noise each night. Once she reached the number one hundred, she sighed a deep breath of relief and dozed off to sleep.

A few blocks away, well after midnight, Mary was still up attempting to outfox a little brown-eyed beauty hyped up on the effects of caffeine and sugar. Earlier in the evening, Miss Charity had hijacked Philip's sweet tea when no one was looking. Now, it was Mary who bore the consequences as she made countless attempts to con her daughter into closing her eyes. The two were cuddled up in the floor of the little girl's room, propped up on pillows and layered up with cozy comforters. Mary had sung every song she knew and recited every story she could recall; her voice was now hoarse and scratchy. She lay still and quiet with the little princess tucked beneath her arm. The moonlight found its way into the room, casting a delicate glow that illuminated the face of Miss. To Mary, in that moment, her daughter was more beautiful than she'd ever been before. Mary watched as Miss Charity's eyes played a game of hopscotch, bouncing around the room in every direction, sometimes followed by a mischievous giggle.

"So, Miss, I take it from your giggles that the angels are in the room with us tonight providing you with some entertainment," Mary spoke, not expecting a response. "I sure do wish I could watch the show with you."

She then considered what the angels might actually look like.

"Do they have wings? Are they flying around? Or do they walk around like we do?" She paused for a few seconds, allowing her eyes to follow wherever the little girl's eyes led.

"Are they all men, or all women, or a mix of both? And are they young or old?" Pinching the end of her daughter's nose, she asked, "Are any of them as adorable as you?" Another quick pause. "Probably not." Mary smiled, and Miss Charity giggled again.

"Do they talk to you? And can they hear your thoughts? Oh, how I wish I could hear your thoughts." A tear escaped her eye. Watching the little, round face beneath her arm, she prayed.

"Lord, thank You for giving me this time with my baby. In the still and quiet, I feel Your presence all around. I am so grateful You send Your angels to guard and protect this sweet princess and our family just as Your word promises." Miss Charity lifted her hand and patted Mary's chest as she continued: "And thank You most of all for choosing me to be her momma. What an honor You have bestowed upon me."

Mary pulled the little one even closer to herself. And at some point, the two finally nodded off to sleep.

The next morning, Philip awoke to find them tightly wrapped on the floor like a knot beneath the mountain of blankets. Careful not to wake them, he tiptoed back down the hall, making his way to the kitchen. He made sure Wills left for school on time and left Tate with instructions to wake her mom by nine in the morning.

"Don't forget to wake her up so you guys can meet me at the Cracker Barrel by ten, all right? You don't want to miss your weekly dose of buttermilk pancakes, do you?" He gave her a big bear hug before heading out the door for work. "I'll see you in a little while." The door closed behind him, leaving the old house eerily quiet. Trudy stood by Tate's side.

"Trudy, do you think this house is spooky when it's quiet?" she asked.

Trudy wagged her tail.

It was not even eight o'clock yet, and Tate hated the prospect of sitting up by herself for an hour while her mother and sister slept. She ran to her room, fetched a blanket and pillow, and dragged them into Miss Charity's room. Within a few minutes, she, too, was fast asleep right beside them. Even Trudy joined them. It was Mary who would open her eyes first at nearly ten o'clock.

"Tate, Miss Charity, what time is it?" she asked, scurrying off to the kitchen. Tate, still groggy, followed behind wrapped in her blanket. "It's nearly ten. Oh, no, we're supposed to be at the Cracker Barrel to meet your daddy."

Mary grabbed the phone, punching in Philip's number.

"Good morning, Mare-Bear! Are you almost here?" he answered, with a chipper voice.

"Chief, you are not going to believe this..."

While Mary was talking to Philip, Bonnie was pulling up in the Cracker Barrel parking lot. She'd already made her run by the Montgomery home, but seeing Mary's car parked in the turnaround, she made a split-second decision to dash out to the Cracker Barrel with the hope of finding Philip all alone. She was right. He was talking on the phone, exiting the front door when she caught up to him.

"Well, Philip, how are you this morning?" she asked, acting completely surprised to see him. It was warm, so she had shimmied herself into a tight-fitting knit blouse with a plunging V-neck and paired the top with an equally fitted pair of capri pants and strappy high heels.

"Well, hey there, Bonnie. I'm on the phone with Mary right now...Mary, guess who's here at the Cracker Barrel? You heard me? Yes, it is Bonnie Cutless," Philip responded.

"Mary says to tell you hello...oh, wait." He held up his finger to Bonnie. "I don't know, honey, but I'll ask her...Bonnie, Mary wants to know if you'll come in and join me for a cup of coffee until she and the kids can get here. They had a late start...unless, of course, you are meeting someone else here." Philip bumbled the words, but Bonnie got the message.

"I'd love nothing more. Tell Mary I'll look forward to visiting with her when she gets here, but until then, I'll try to be good company for you." Bonnie placed her hand on Philip's shoulder and allowed it to run down his arm as she passed by him. "I'll go reserve a big table for all of us."

Philip hated his eyes. Why did he allow them to follow Bonnie's curves? She caught his reflection in the door as she opened it. *He may call himself a Christian, but he's still a man*, she thought to herself.

"Philip? Are you still there?" Mary questioned.

"Yeah, Mary, I'm still here. Hurry up and get here; Bonnie has gone in to get us all a table," he answered while straightening his tie and making a fuss over his hair, using his own reflection in the big window as he wondered why he suddenly cared about how he looked.

"I'll be there in a jiff; just make sure you are very nice to her. I really think she's trying to change but just doesn't know how to go about it. This may be a huge step in the right direction," Mary encouraged him.

Philip entered the restaurant and found Bonnie at a corner table. She patted the table, encouraging Philip to sit directly across from her. He sat down. The waitress brought him a coffee and Bonnie a glass of ice water. The two began to engage in conversation.

"How often do you work out, Philip?" she asked.

"How did you know I work out?" He returned her question with one of his own in a joking way.

"Let's just say I can tell. But I'm not guilty of checking you out or anything." Bonnie shot him a wink and a smile.

"Uhhhm, yeah." He recovered. "I go to the gym whenever I can. It's not easy, though, because Mary needs me to get home and help out with the kids, especially with Miss Charity," he answered, getting the subject back on his family but beginning to wonder if she was flirting with him. *No, that's silly*, he thought to himself.

After a few minutes, Bonnie deliberately spilled some water on her blouse while taking a sip. "Oh, look at me, clumsy as ever." She took her napkin and began to dab the water off her right breast, pulling her shirt down each time she brushed at it, revealing her lacy bra. She looked back up at Philip, whose jaw was wide open. "Did I get it all?" she asked, pulling her blouse tight with both hands. "This is so embarrassing."

"Yep, I think you got it," Philip answered, his mouth completely dry and his feet numb. "Will you excuse me for a moment, Bonnie? I'm going to call Mary and see how close they are to getting here so I can make sure to go out and help her get Tate and the baby into the restaurant."

As he walked away, Bonnie took out her purse and freshened her lipstick. "Oh, Philip Montgomery, you dirty, dirty boy."

Chapter 24

Just before nightfall, the entire Montgomery family was seated around the table after finishing dinner with GiGi, Poppy, and Crew.

"Wills," Philip asked, "why don't you and Crew take your sisters out in the backyard for a little while to get them some fresh air before bedtime?" Twisting Wills's arm a bit, he added: "Tate, wouldn't you like to beat the guys again in a game of horse?"

After seeing that Tate and the boys were well into their competition and making sure Miss Charity was happily digging in some pine mulch, Philip began: "All right, I have got to talk to y'all about something very disturbing."

Now concerned, Mary, who was already busy gathering the dishes, placed them back down on the table and took her seat. "Sure, Chief, what is it?"

Philip cleared his throat, crossed his arms, and threw it out on the table to be discussed.

"It's about Bonnie. She came on to me today at the Cracker Barrel."

"Came on to you?" GiGi drew her chin back so far into her neck, it looked like her face was attached to her shoulders. "Oh my Lord, what has that woman done now?"

Philip, relieved to know at least one person was buying into his story, pulled up his own seat to the table. "Well, you know how Mary was up late last night with Miss Charity?"

GiGi interrupted with a cackle: "Yeah, she told us about how that little bugger got into your tea last night."

"Because of that, she overslept this morning and was late getting to the restaurant. Bonnie, for some strange reason, just so happened to be there and ended up sitting at the table with me until Mary could get there." Philip leaned over the table, eyes so wide they looked like they might pop clear out of his head, and softened his voice to a whisper: "I believe she flashed her breasts at me."

It didn't take a millisecond for GiGi to raise her hands up in the air: "I knew it, I knew it, I knew it! She planted that kiss on his cheek at church for all of us to see. She is after you, Philip, and she is a dangerous kind of woman."

"The most dangerous kind of woman," Poppy wholeheartedly agreed.

Mary was incredulous: "You have to be kidding me. There is no way you all actually believe Bonnie has the hots for the Chief."

"Why wouldn't she have the hots for him?" Poppy asked. "Her husband is never around, and a woman like that is surely gonna find somebody to chase around. Might as well be your husband."

206

Mary had to reign in her family before they went off on a wild goose chase. "From what I understand, her husband travels a lot for the bank. Their marriage might be strained, but that doesn't mean Bonnie is after my husband. You all are being ridiculous, and with Crew right out there in the backyard. I'd be ashamed."

"Mary, you are as blind as a possum on a country road in the dead of night," GiGi answered, wagging that all-too-familiar finger at her daughter. Then, pretending to bow her head for prayer, the old bird folded her hands and spoke with the best-sounding religious voice she could muster: "Jesus, Lord help us all; open the eyes of the blind, and let her see the devil's ways!"

Ignoring his wife's dramatic performance, Poppy chimed in: "Philip, why don't you tell us everything that happened today?"

Philip carefully recounted the entire experience, hoping to sway Mary's mind about Bonnie's intentions toward him. It didn't work. Mary insisted, "But when I arrived at the restaurant with Tate and Miss Charity, Bonnie was as nice as pie to me, an absolute doll. We can't expect her to act like we do or to dress like we do. Who knows if she's ever been taught about honoring the Lord with her words, her body, and her actions? I bet she hasn't. You all are expecting way too much out of her and are reading something into this that just isn't there."

She was speaking with great certainty and authority until her mother butted in: "Or maybe you are underestimating her. Have you considered that?"

"Look out in the backyard at Crew so happy playing ball with Tate and Wills, showing such kindness to our little Miss. I turned my back on him and forgot he was lost. I expected him to act like a follower of God when he didn't even know God." Mary's emotions grew as she continued. "I won't make that same mistake with his momma. I am just going to love her with no judgment."

Philip listened and understood his wife's point of view; however, he remained unsettled about his own predicament with Bonnie.

"Mare-Bear," he said, "I'm telling you, I have a feeling she is not going to give up. I'm afraid your mom is right. You might be underestimating her."

His one last attempt fell on deaf ears: "No, I don't think so, Philip. Sin is sin. I battle sin myself every single day. Bonnie Cutless is no more a sinner than you or me. She's just missing the Redeemer. We need to love her, be Jesus to her, and..."

But before Mary could continue, GiGi stopped her dead in her tracks: "Oh, shut up the church speak and listen to your husband. You are being so unfair to him. What if this was a man hitting on you?"

"What do you want me to say, Mom? Give her the cold shoulder...put up the walls...turn her away...?"

GiGi didn't hesitate: "Yes, honey, that's exactly what you should be saying!"

"Did Jesus shy away from the woman at the well?" Mary asked.

"Is Philip Jesus?" GiGi returned.

"No, my husband is not Jesus. But I trust him completely."

Poppy muttered again: "Well, if he ain't Jesus, he's just a man. And to expect him to handle a woman like the one that was at the well with Jesus, well, I don't know how wise that is." Turning to Philip, she added, "No offense to you at all, son."

Philip kind of smiled. Well, he gave one of his half smiles. And as he listened to the exchange, he felt ashamed for feeling any attraction at all to Bonnie and unworthy of his wife's great trust.

"Listen, maybe I have made too big a deal out of this, Mare-Bear. I think you are right. Bonnie is a wandering, lost soul...probably angry her husband is never around...frustrated she doesn't have a better relationship with her son...and she has obviously been seduced by the trappings of this world, focusing more on outer beauty and overt sexuality than inner beauty and purity. I don't know why her behavior caught me so off guard when I should have expected it. Of course you can trust me."

"Seduced by the trappings of this world?" GiGi piped in again. "Did you really just say that mumbo jumbo? You sound like one of those greasy, late-night preachers on the cable TV station."

Philip responded by raising his eyebrows. She continued, allowing her eyes to bore right into her son-in-law: "I don't know who or what has seduced Bonnie Cutless. I don't even give a hoot if she has or has not been seduced, but I have a strong feeling she is going to seduce you. King David was a man after God's own heart, and he came crashing down like a giant oak in the forest. *Timberrrrr!*" she cried. "Bathsheba was the one with the axe that cut him down. Are you a better man than King David?"

"Mother, Philip and I have a strong and happy marriage. Think of all the years we've been together, and have a little faith in us. Give us some credit," Mary answered for Philip.

"I'm not denying any of that, but remember, it wasn't that long ago that you and the Chief had a little chink in your mighty marriage armor over Crew. Even strong marriages can sometimes break."

"I would hardly call it a chink," Mary quipped.

"It doesn't matter what you'd call it. The point is, your marriage is not indestructible."

"So, what you are saying is Philip is going to dump me and our kids to go have a fling with Bonnie?

That's how much you believe in the father of your grandchildren?" Mary was getting angrier by the minute and chose not to hide it any longer. Her face was red, and her hands shook. "Maybe you and Pops need to go on home. You are really upsetting me."

"I've got one more thing to say, and then we'll leave. Two words. And, Philip, you better listen to them. Joseph fled."

GiGi shot from her seat like a rocket, marched to the table standing near the front door, took hold of her purse with a swoop of her arm, and proceeded out the door while giving out one final holler: "Joseph fled!" Then she slammed the door hard, rattling the house.

Poppy put his arm around Mary, trying to bring her some comfort. "Now just calm down and think about this. Your momma loves you so much. She's just worried; that's all." He gave a chuckle while planting a soft kiss on the side of his daughter's head. "I'm going to say good-bye to the kids, and then I'll just walk around the house and be out of here. That will hopefully give your momma a chance to simmer down a bit."

"Do you agree with her?" Mary asked, hoping he didn't.

Poppy turned his back to Mary, took a few steps toward the back door, and considered carefully how to respond. "I have to be honest," he said, his back still to Mary as he watched the children

laughing and playing through the back window,
"I'm concerned too." Dipping his head, he slipped
out the back door, closing it softly behind him.

The ride home, Pops figured, would be a long one,
so he decided to give GiGi a few extra minutes to
cool down in the car.

"You guys think you can take on an old man at a
game of horse?" he asked the small group. Miss
Charity, hearing Poppy's voice, came running full
sprint and threw her arms around his legs. Tate's
face brightened up with a big smile. "Not only will
we take you on; we'll beat you!"

Poppy had been a local basketball star during his
heyday at what was now Lee University. The
sprawling college campus sat across the street,
very near the Montgomery home. He bantered on
with Tate:

"Well, that would be the first time, but I reckon'
there's always a first time for just about
everything."

As he made his way to the makeshift basketball
court, which amounted to a concrete slab with a
regulation-sized goal, Miss Charity still clung tightly
to his right leg. "If little Miss keeps on hanging on
to my leg like this, you guys just might have a
chance today."

"Excuses, excuses," Wills heckled. "Surely a guy
who averaged more than thirty points a game
before the three-point shot had ever been thought

up can beat a bunch of kids at a shooting game, even with a five-year-old appendage hanging on his leg."

Poppy retorted while patting the humidity-induced curls on Miss Charity's head, "You call it an appendage, but I'll call it an unfair advantage for me. She's my good-luck charm!"

Miss Charity didn't understand what her Poppy was saying, but she deciphered the kind tone in his voice and knew he was pleased with her. In response, she held on even tighter. Poppy shot the first ball from the top of the key, an area that had been carefully marked by a piece of Tate's sidewalk chalk. The ball made a swooshing sound as it found nothing but net.

Poppy had been married to GiGi for more than forty years, which was enough time for him to know she was always up to something. When she slammed the front door of Mary's home, she simultaneously made up her mind to walk a few blocks. It was time to pay Bonnie a little visit.

Chapter 25

Bonnie was propped up with pillows reading notes in the margin of Mary's Bible when she heard a knock at the front door. Deciding it was probably a student trying to raise money for a summer sports program or a Jehovah's Witness trying to convert her, she remained in her bed, ignoring the sound. But then she heard it again, this time with a high-pitched southern drawl:

"Bonnie, I know you're in there, and I'm gonna keep on knockin' until you come to this door!"

It was a female's voice, possibly familiar. Making a dash for her closet, the blond beauty sans makeup pulled a sweatshirt over her tank and made her way to the door in bare feet. Rounding the corner at the end of the hallway, she saw the woman. It was GiGi.

"What in God's name are you doing here?" she asked, after opening the door.

GiGi answered, pointing her index finger, and taking note of the black Bible in Bonnie's hand at the same time: "I'll tell you what I'm doing here. I'm here to give you a warning!"

"A warning?" The beauty's eyes lit up as she purposefully teased. "This wouldn't have anything to do with my new boyfriend, would it?"

GiGi's jaw dropped open. She stood looking dumbstruck. Her face unabashedly showed fury, but she remained silent, allowing Bonnie to continue and hoping like heck she wasn't talking about her son-in-law.

"You do know about Philip and me, right? That is why you've come knocking on my door?" Bonnie's voice held no sign of alarm; the two glasses of wine had effectively cut out all signs of uneasiness. The woman's voice was smooth and eerily sensual.

GiGi paused to take a deep breath, realizing she was not near as calm and in control as her counterpart. Preparing to give Bonnie a mouthful, she raised her hand and opened her mouth, but the devil woman stalled her with a *"Stop!* Save your breath, old bat...what's going on between Philip and me is our business and certainly none of yours. Now be a good girl, pull up all your sags and bags, and go home."

GiGi heard the click of the deadbolt just as the red, wooden door closed in her face. She could have pounded the door and screamed. She wanted to do much more than that. However, she turned and walked back to Mary's and Philip's house. She was steaming yet satisfied she'd gathered the information she was after.

Back at the house, Poppy had just come around to the car after beating the grandkids handily at a game of horse and was surprised to find that GiGi was not in the car waiting for him as he'd expected. Knowing his wife's nature as well as the lines marking the palms of his hands, he began making his way toward Bonnie's house when he caught a faint glimpse of her through the bushes, walking toward him. Picking up his pace, he rushed to greet her.

"What have you done?" he asked, nearly out of breath. GiGi's strides were long and fast; Poppy turned to walk alongside his bride, who appeared to be on a mission.

"Since you came out to find old sags and bags and seemed to know the direction to look, I'm guessing you know exactly what I've done," she answered sharply.

"I can't believe this! You actually went to Bonnie's house and confronted her?" Poppy's shock didn't deter GiGi one bit.

"Oh, I went there to put the fear of the ever-loving God into that hussy, but she is pretty much the one who put me in my place. And that ain't easy to do."

Poppy wanted details. "What happened?"

"Is Crew still at the house?" she asked.

"Yes, he's still out back shooting ball."

"I don't want him to hear anything, so let's get in the car and get out of here. I'll tell you all about it on the way home."

GiGi couldn't wait to tell Poppy every detail of the short conversation, and she began as soon as they drove away. Her big exclamation came as she finished.

"But do you know what's really creepy?" she asked.

"You mean there's something creepier than what you've just told me?" Poppy's eyes were fixed on the red light before him.

"That bleached-blond demon has Mary's Bible."

After whipping his head just about off his shoulders, Poppy shouted, "What are you saying?"

"Yeah, I'd know that old, worn-out Bible anywhere. Somehow Satan's seed has gotten her slimy hands on Mary's Bible. And I'm one hundred percent sure it's not because she's looking for God."

The light turned green. Poppy gave his car a tap of gas so they could start moving again. His wife was known for being quite an instigator, dramatic at times, but not this time. He had a sinking feeling.

"How on earth did she get hold of Mary's Bible?" he asked as several possibilities ran through his mind, his southern drawl as pronounced as ever.

GiGi started digging her cell phone out of her purse. "Praise God you actually believe me; that's a first."

"You gonna call Mary and let her know?"

"Nope, I'm going to send her a text message so she can think on it awhile. I'll let her know we'll be there first thing in the morning, after Wills has left for school, to give her all the details."

Poppy quickly added: "Tell her I'll stop by the bakery and get some doughnuts."

Pursing her lips, GiGi shot Poppy the look of death: "Only you would think of doughnuts at a time like this. The devil has Mary's Bible. God only knows how she got it. Maybe she even broke into their house and stole it! And here you are thinking about doughnuts? This is just the cherry on top of my day, a picture of the sin of gluttony on display. You need prayer—serious, down-on-your-knees prayer."

Poppy kept his eyes on the road, paying GiGi's words no attention. The last words in her text to Mary were: "Poppy says he'll bring doughnuts in the morning. We should all be fasting and praying, preparing to anoint your house with holy oil, but all he can think about is eating. Pray for your daddy, honey."

Chapter 26

The next morning couldn't come fast enough for GiGi. She was not sure whether she'd slept at all. When they arrived, Philip and Mary were seated at the kitchen table drinking coffee. Mary rose and greeted them both with hugs.

"Y'all try to be quiet. I let Tate and Miss Charity sleep in this morning so we could talk."

GiGi made a beeline for the kitchen, pouring two cups of coffee as Poppy sheepishly placed the box of doughnuts on the table.

"Go ahead and open that box, you glutton!" she fired off, forgetting to keep her voice down. "Jesus is reading your mind right now, and He knows you are thinking about those doughnuts instead of what you ought to be thinking about, so you might as well eat 'em. You're sinning anyway, standing over that box obsessing about what's inside."

Mary, reaching for the box and opening it, slid it toward her father: "Mom, don't talk so loud! And, Dad, don't listen to Miss Size-Six Grandma. She's just angry because if she eats one, she might gain a pound and won't be able to shimmy into those tight jeans anymore."

Poppy grabbed two, sat back in the chair, and decided to let his wife know he was enjoying every bite. GiGi took her place at the table, gave her husband an eye roll, and began filling Mary and Philip in on her visit to Bonnie's house the night before.

Philip turned to his wife. "What do you think?"

"Besides the fact that my mother is a crazy lady?" Mary couldn't get over the fact that her mother had walked to Bonnie's house and taken her head on.

GiGi answered, "Yes, besides that. Now c'mon, we have to devise a plan before the children wake up. Really, Mary, what do you think?"

"Daddy, do you buy into Mom's story?" she asked, again hoping he would see things the way she did.

Poppy finished chewing the last bite of the first doughnut and took a sip of coffee before answering. "As strange as it all sounds, I do. I don't necessarily think Bonnie is possessed by the devil, but she does give me the willies. And I think both your mom and I would be able to identify your Bible anywhere. You've had that thing since you were a kid."

Shaking her head, Mary blurted out: "OK, you want to know what I think? I think the devil has possessed all of you! It's like I've already told you; Bonnie is a lost soul who needs Jesus. She is coming to church now, where she might actually find salvation, and the devil has got you all paranoid about her. If you keep pushing her away, acting judgmental and marching up to her house to attack her..." Mary gave her mom a frightful glare. "Mother, I am talking mostly to you! If you keep this up, the devil will win, and Bonnie's soul will be lost forever. And it will all be your fault because you keep getting in the way of the Holy Spirit!"

Philip broke in: "Listen, Mary..."

"Listen to what?" she asked. "Listen to my momma say Bonnie has the hots for you and is about to destroy our family? That she has broken into our home to steal my Bible, which she just so happened to have in her hands last night when my completely sane mother"—Mary made quotation marks with her fingers as she spewed those last three words—"showed up at her house on a rampage? Is that what you want me to listen to, Chief?"

Mary drilled them with sarcasm, determined to make her point even if they found it offensive; but GiGi wasn't budging. She was undisturbed by her daughter's tirade and sincerely interested in stopping Bonnie before things spiraled out of control.

"Yes, Mary, that is precisely what we want you to listen to. Instead of using this precious time arguing, let's all figure out how she broke into this house and what her next move is going to be."

Philip, seeing his wife visibly frustrated, made another attempt to get through to her.

"Mare-Bear, I know you are still feeling guilty about rejecting Crew, and you don't want to make the same mistake with his mom. I get that and think your parents do too…"

Before he could finish his thought, however, he heard the front door open and close. The four turned at once to see Viv bustling in.

"Did I miss anything?" she asked, pulling out a chair and joining them around the kitchen table. "I am so sorry I'm running late; I overslept. I started taking melatonin recently, and it makes me sleep like a baby. Anyway, have you come up with a plan to trap the thief and throw cold water on her mojo?"

"Oh, great…so glad Mother has spread the gossip through town now," Mary responded. "What is mojo?"

Viv looked at her sister with surprise. "First, I am not the town's rumor mill, thank you very much. Second, mojo is what the oversexed stank Bonnie Cutless is shooting toward your hubby. And third, fix me a cup of coffee already."

"You know what?" Mary stood, incensed. "You've all decided Bonnie is a whacko, and what you can't see is that you all have turned into a bunch of whackos. I'm not going to be able to convince you otherwise, so I'm going to take my shower and get dressed before my babies get up." Mary made her way to the kitchen. Placing her cup in the sink, she looked up at Viv. "Fix your own cup of coffee." Then, walking toward her bedroom, she added,

"Make your plans to bring down the devilish Delilah; I sure won't be a part of it."

With Mary out of the room, Poppy, GiGi, Philip, and Viv did have a serious discussion. The four were certain Bonnie was up to something, and they feared the unwitting, ever-trusting Mary was her primary target.

Chapter 27

Bonnie knew Mary's mother was on to her, so she didn't have the luxury of time on her side. When she awoke, she immediately began to put her next plan of action into motion. Stealing Mary's physical possessions had been child's play; stealing her husband would require woman's work. As she stood looking at herself in the mirror, Bonnie was pleased with how good the years had been to her. Her face was void of lines and creases, her hair still thick and full of life, and her body taut with muscle. She sang: "Homely Mary had a man, had a man, had a man...homely Mary had a man 'til Bonnie formed her plan."

To get ready for the day ahead of her, Bonnie took a nice, long bubble bath, continuing to hum the tune of "Mary Had a Little Lamb" as she marked each moment of the day in her mind. She would not allow herself to get off course. Then, ducking her hands down into the soapy water, she allowed her hands to run up and down her naked body, taking care to feel every nuance. And just before exiting the claw-foot tub, in the most sultry voice she could muster, she spoke: "Philip Montgomery, you lucky man, you have no idea what's coming to you!"

It was time to put her plan into action.

Bonnie finally entered Philip's office at five thirty in the afternoon. The fact that she could walk in on the half hour was a sign to her that things were going to go well, especially since she had sat across the street for more than an hour, patiently waiting for the last of his employees to leave.

"Good old Philip," she thought out loud, "he is as reliable as they come, which should make this all the more interesting."

Philip's business sat on Keith Street, and his office was in the front of the building with a window overlooking the busy street. Had he been paying attention, he would have noticed Bonnie long before she entered the room.

"Philip...um, hey...can I come in and bother you for a minute?" she asked, gently giving a tap on the door of his office.

Instinct made him zip around in his chair, not giving his brain time to process the sound of the voice.

"Oh my gosh, Bonnie. You scared me there for a second," he managed to say, his heart now pulverizing his chest wall.

Wearing a short, stretchy, candy-apple-red dress that barely covered her derriere, Bonnie stood in six-inch heels the same color. Her legs looked forever long. "I hoped I'd find you here. I need to speak with you about Mary's mother if you could give me just a tiny little second of your time."

"Sure, um, yeah, have a seat."

He wondered what else he could say to a woman who was only asking for a second of his time, but all the while his mother-in-law's words drummed in his head: "Flee, Joseph! Flee, Joseph!"

The blonde with the mile-long legs pulled the wing-backed chair around, carefully centering it in front of Philip's chunky mahogany desk. And when she'd positioned it the way she wanted it, she slowly took a seat.

"I know you're a very busy man, running this successful business and all," she flattered him, "so I appreciate your letting me surprise you with a visit."

Philip said nothing but continued to think of a polite way to weasel his way out of the situation. His cell phone sat on the desk in front of him, so he began to pray in his head: "Lord, please have Mary call me." But the phone didn't ring.

"I didn't feel comfortable talking to Mary about this since it has to do with her mother...you know...I don't want to cause any trouble between them. I hope you can help me, Philip."

Bonnie leaned back in the chair, stopped speaking, and waited for him to respond.

"I'll try to help you if I can." Philip wrung his hands, bit his lip, and managed to ask, "What's the problem?"

Of course, he knew full well his mother-in-law had made a visit to Bonnie's house the night before, and the woman would likely die when she found out what that visit had now caused.

Bonnie, seeing she finally had Philip's full attention, uncrossed her legs, pulling her knees several inches apart. Philip's eyes instinctively followed the movement.

"The strangest thing happened last night. Your mother-in-law took me completely off guard. You're really not going to believe this…"

Bonnie recounted GiGi's visit to her home, feigning surprise that the elder woman would have such negative feelings toward her.

"I don't know why she doesn't like me, because I've honestly tried to be nice to her…"

She talked and talked, while Philip only heard bits and pieces, just enough to gather the general gist of what she was saying. The entire time, however, he couldn't get over the fact that the most beautiful woman in town was seated before him, legs spread, with no sign of panties.

At the same time, Mary was cooking dinner while Tate, Miss Charity, Wills, and Crew hung out in the backyard. Looking out the kitchen window, she could see Tate pushing her little sister in the swing while Wills and Crew threw the football. She checked the time, and it was getting close to six o'clock. "The Chief should be home soon," she said to Trudy, who was lying at her feet, hoping for a nibble of shepherd's pie, Wills's favorite dish. The distinct aroma of meat cooking kept her black, furry friend as close as a shadow to Mary in the kitchen. It was several minutes later, when Miss Charity tugged at her blouse signing the word *eat*, that Mary decided to make a call to Philip.

"Hey, I thought you were out swinging with your buddy?" she asked, as the little Miss repeatedly put her fingers to her mouth and then pulled them away with quick rhythm. "All right, I get it. You're hungry and ready to eat. Let's call Daddy and see how much longer he's going to be, OK?"

Mary lifted her little girl up to sit on the kitchen counter and dialed Philip's number from her cell phone. What she and Miss Charity could not see was the demon seated on the counter right next to them. Unbridled muscles bulged beneath his black V-neck T-shirt, and his emerald-green eyes bored into those belonging to the woman he aimed to crush.

"That's odd," she said, directing her words more toward the cell phone than to her daughter. "Every time I press call on the phone, the call ends."

Miss Charity, seeing her mom a bit concerned, brought levity and began to giggle.

Mary teased her: "This isn't funny. I've tried to call your daddy three times so we can get down to the business of filling that grumbly tummy of yours with some dinner, but this silly phone keeps cutting off my call before he can answer."

Neither Mary nor the little Miss could see the demon's finger manipulating the phone. Each time Mary pressed the call button, he matched her by pressing the end button. Her mission was fruitless.

The little girl continued her giggles, now pointing her finger across the room at the angel of light only she could see. He made silly faces and sounds, completely cracking his little buddy up. Mary intuitively turned in the direction the little finger pointed. "Is it one of your angels again?" she asked. "Let me put you down so you can go play with your friend!"

Mary assisted the girl in pigtails off the counter and began to dial yet again. The angel made his way across the kitchen and now stood, facing the demon, with Miss Charity at his side.

"Better luck next time," he said.

The demon pulled back his arm, which displayed a bicep the size of Mary's thigh, and brought his fist down hard toward the top of Mary's head. As if hitting an invisible wall, contact was stopped only millimeters from the demon's intended blow. She was protected. Untouchable. And both the angel and demon knew it. The angel, acting uninterested in his counterpart, sat on the floor with Miss Charity, who quickly plopped down on the floor facing him. As Mary listened to Philip's line ring, she glanced down, taking note of her little cutie, legs folded, on the floor.

The angel continued the one-sided conversation:

"It stinks losing a battle, doesn't it? You have no power over Mary and the blessed one, so be a good demon and get out of here. Oh, but one more thing before you go. Next time, make sure you remember it is Philip you have been given permission to test." His voice then thundered: "*Leave Mary and Miss Charity alone!*" And within the span of a blink, the dark one disappeared.

Miss Charity was disturbed by her angel's strong voice and sought reassurance, flashing her puppy-dog eyes up at him, questioning if all was all right. Grinning, he reached out to give her some big tickles on her ribs. His voice, now smooth as butter, put her at ease: "Oh, don't you worry about anything, little love...your angel is just doing his job and protecting you from all kinds of harm. We're going to get through this together, all right?"

"Hey, Mary," Philip answered his phone.

"Hey, baby! Where are you? A little somebody wanted me to call and letcha know she is nearly starving and ready to eat." Mary bent down next to her daughter, who was now having a full-on giggling session with her angel. His tickles were more than the little one could take.

Philip didn't respond, so she continued: "Well, I guess she doesn't really sound like she's very hungry, does she? Can you hear her?" Miss Charity's laughter must have been contagious, because Mary suddenly burst out into giggles too.

Philip remained silent.

"Philip." Mary caught her breath from all the cackling. "Are you there, honey?" For some reason, his not answering her made Mary laugh even harder.

"Yeah, I'm here. I'll be home in twenty minutes...I just have to wrap up one more thing before I leave," he answered, and then he quickly ended the call without saying good-bye. Mary didn't even notice. Instead, she lay down in the floor on her back and continued to laugh out loud with her little girl.

"What is so freaking funny?" she asked, pulling Miss Charity over to her and up under her arm. "Why are we so hysterical? Tell me, please!"

And as the two continued to giggle until catching a breath was hard to do, the angel gave a big chuckle himself before going away.

Turning his chair to face the open window behind him, Mary's husband didn't share his wife's exuberance. Feeling much regret, he watched through his office window as Bonnie opened her car door and climbed in. And as soon as he knew she had driven safely out of sight, he spun his chair around to again face his desk before pounding it hard with both fists. "What is wrong with you,

Philip?" His voice filled the space each time his hands met the wooden table. "Why did you sit here like an idiot and say nothing?"

Bringing his elbows down to the desk, he covered his face with the hands that had always held Mary's. "God, forgive me. Please, God, forgive me. I should have sent that woman away or left my office as soon as she walked in. I know better. Oh, boy, do I know better. I admit it, Lord; I am attracted to Bonnie. Please, will You take that from me and protect my marriage from her advances? I love my wife and my family and don't want to hurt them. Oh, God, I wouldn't hurt them for anything. Thank You for my family, Father...please, forgive me."

It took Philip thirty minutes to get home instead of the projected twenty, because he made a quick stop by the grocery store. When he and Mary were still teenagers, he used to buy her a pack of SweeTarts candy and ask: "A SweeTart for my sweetheart?" Even though it teetered on making him feel a bit nerdy, she loved it, so he had continued it throughout their marriage. Today, he thought, was a perfect day to bring Mary a pack of SweeTarts.

Cracking the door, Philip crooned: "Maaaary, how do I love thee? Let me count the ways! My bounty is as boundless as the sea...my love as deep; the more I give to thee..."

Mary quickly answered back, "Get in here, you big poet!"

Philip, in response to her happy voice, bounded through the door with the pack of SweeTarts in one hand and a mix of colorful, fresh flowers in the other, nearly knocking her over with enthusiasm as he hugged her. Planting a kiss on her neck, he then asked, "SweeTart for my sweetheart?" and pulled a roll of candy out for her to see, along with the flowers.

Mary took a step back and teased, "How many times have I told you it is not proper to mix Elizabeth Barrett Browning up with Shakespeare?" Grabbing the sweet treat, she broke the roll in half and helped herself to a purple one, her favorite flavor.

"Wow, aren't you lucky to have such a flirt for a husband, Mary?" His stomach took a leap to his throat when he heard the familiar voice coming from the great-room area.

"C'mon, Chief, look who came by for a visit." Mary, pulling her husband by the arm, directed him toward the voice. "Bonnie had just finished working out at the gym, was getting ready to pass our house on the way home, and decided to stop by for a quick visit. I'm so happy to see her...aren't you?"

Bonnie loved a game of cat and mouse. "I hope you don't mind, Philip," she said, shooting him a knowing grin with eyes that purposefully drew him, every word sounding remarkably seductive to him. "Mary has invited me to stay for dinner, and I've accepted. I'm hoping this will help me mend my relationship with Crew, since I know he eats here with you guys nearly every evening."

Philip was stunned. Not only was Bonnie Cutless seated on the sofa in his great room, but what was even more surprising to him was the fact that she was wearing leggings, athletic shoes, and a T-shirt. Where had she stashed the red dress and heels?

"Of course, that is fine with me," Philip replied nervously. "I'm going to go put on some jeans, Mare-Bear, and will be right back. Dinner smells wonderful, by the way!" He jetted out of the room like his butt was on fire. Once safely in the closet, he pulled out his cell phone and made a quick call.

"GiGi," he whispered, "I need you and Poppy to stop by as soon as you can get here. I can't explain right now, but Bonnie has shown up over here, and I need some backup."

Chapter 28

Mary's parents had no idea what they would be in for when they arrived at the house on Ocoee Street, but nonetheless, they wrapped up what was left of their barely eaten dinner, threw it into the fridge, and made their way to rescue their daughter's family from the devil woman.

"Knock, knock!" sang the shrill voice of GiGi just before she entered the room wearing a crisp, white button-down paired with hot-pink Bermuda shorts and flip-flops. When she rounded the corner, she found the entire family seated around the table with Bonnie and Crew.

Tate, surprised to see her grandmother, rushed to give her a big hug. "GiGi!"

"Lord, child, you smell like dirt." GiGi wrinkled her nose, returning the hug with a slight pat on Tate's back.

The preteen didn't care; she went on wrapping her arms tightly around GiGi's neck. "That's because we've been playing outside. You do know I'm still a kid, right?"

Wills got up to greet his grandmother too, wrapping his long arms around both her and Tate. "Where's Pops?"

"Oh, he should be right behind me," she answered as Tate broke loose, darting off to look for him. Within seconds, she returned holding the hands of both Poppy and Aunt Viv.

Mary stood graciously, greeting them all. "I wasn't expecting you." She gave them hugs. "I hope I have enough food for everyone, but if not, Chief can order some pizza!"

Her father quickly put her concerns to rest: "Oh, no, we didn't come to eat. We're just going out to the mall to help Viv find herself a new dress for this weekend."

"She's got a hot date with that lawyer friend of hers," GiGi butted in. "Maybe he's the one!"

Viv pulled a seat up to the table. "Look who's here, Momma! How are you, Bonnie?" she asked.

"I am just finishing up this incredible feast Mary prepared," Bonnie replied, seeming unbothered by those who had just showed up. Wiping the corners of her mouth with a napkin, she continued: "But I was just about to leave, so you all arrived just in time. GiGi, dear, you can have my seat!"

As Bonnie stood to gather her dish, Mary reached, taking hold of her arm. "No, please don't leave."

Pausing for a brief moment, Bonnie allowed her eyes to linger on Mary's face. She appeared to be sincere. "You have been so kind to allow me to share this meal with your family and my Crew."

Turning to her son, she added, "I hope this will be the beginning of a brand-new relationship for us. Maybe you and I can be a family like the Montgomerys."

She pretended to get emotional while carrying her dish to the kitchen. Crew didn't know how to respond, so he didn't say anything at all. Underneath the table, Wills was kicking his leg.

As for GiGi, she sat in the now-empty seat and waved her hand. "Bye-bye, Bonnie!" she sang, again with the shrill voice, as Mary walked her guest to the door.

When everyone had finished eating, Philip slipped Wills some cash and asked him to take Crew and Tate down to the Dairy Kreme for an upside-down banana split, Wills's favorite dessert in town. He was more than happy to oblige, so the three took off in a flash.

"Guys, we need to have another serious discussion," he began.

Mary interrupted: "Wait, I thought my parents and Viv were on the way to the mall."

"That was just a ploy," GiGi said with a huff. "Philip called us and asked us to come."

Mary was visibly surprised by the news.

"Mary," Philip continued, "Bonnie showed up at my office today. When you called me, she was there."

"Yes, I know." Mary, becoming agitated, crossed her legs and folded her arms. "She told me she stopped by your office to talk about Mom's visit to her house. She came to talk to you about it first because she was afraid it might humiliate me to find out my mother is a crazy lady!" Glancing at GiGi, she added, "Don't worry; I told her that news was no shock to me!"

"Good Lord, Mary, don't you find it odd that she'd go talk to Philip at his office about something personal like this? She barely knows him!" GiGi responded, aghast.

"Barely knows him? She's been coming to church and sees Philip is a church leader. She probably went to him just like someone would go to Preacher Walker for advice. She told me Philip encouraged her to come by the house to talk to me about it."

"OK, that never happened." Philip blurted out the words, feeling unsettled about his wife's conversation with Bonnie. "She showed up at my office wearing this very tight, very short, red dress...and these spiked high heels...and no sign of underwear...and she pulled up a chair in front of my desk...spread her legs like this...and..." Acting out the scene, Philip had just spread his legs open when Mary jumped in:

"Hold on, Chief! What time did Bonnie come by your office today?"

"I don't know exactly what time it was, but it must have been sometime around five thirty, because I was getting ready to leave when she showed up."

"And she arrived here less than an hour later wearing her workout clothes, just coming from the gym. That seems odd, doesn't it?"

GiGi, Poppy, and Viv said nothing. What could they say? The three of them were on Philip's side, but Mary seemed to be on the side of Bonnie. Miss Charity, noting the tension in the room, waddled over and scrunched herself in between her grandparents. GiGi took one of the little girl's bare feet in her hands; it was dirty from the hours spent outside. As Philip and Mary talked, she rubbed each tiny toe.

"Sure, odd would be one way to describe it." Philip's voice grew louder with each word that followed. "The woman is a nutcase would be another! She obviously planned the whole thing out and is very good at covering her tracks!"

"And about the underwear," Mary butted in, "why were you looking?"

"She flashed me! Have you ever been flashed by someone, Mary? You can't look away when you're being flashed, because you aren't expecting it! Being flashed comes as a surprise!"

GiGi jumped in: "That is the God's honest truth, honey." She continued to rub the little one's feet as she spoke. "Do you remember when that teenage boy streaked across the field in that tiny Speedo at the homecoming game this year? I looked, you looked...the whole darned crowd looked! And let's face it, that itty-bitty Speedo was barely covering the boy's jewels. I can still picture it in my mind."

Viv added, "It's true. No matter how hard we tried, we couldn't look away. We watched him run the whole length of that field. If he'd been bare naked, I don't think it would've made a difference."

"GiGi and Viv are right!" Poppy added. "I even looked at that poor boy running across the field half naked. I can still see his big old white belly flopping up and down over that Speedo. If it hadn't been for him wearing a full Obama mask, he would've gotten expelled. Nobody ever found out who he was, did they, Philip?"

"Please don't change the subject, Pops!" Mary insisted. "Who cares about the kid who streaked at the homecoming game? My husband is accusing Bonnie of flashing him. You all saw her; was she wearing a short, red dress?"

GiGi put Miss Charity's foot back down on the couch, looked up, and answered: "Philip said the devil woman showed up in a short, red dress and flashed him. I heard him clear as day, and you did too. So yes, duh, I believe him."

"I believe him too," Viv said.

Mary, now flustered and angry, could barely get her words out fast enough: "So Bonnie is now a full-time flasher. Wow! Do you all hear what you are accusing this woman of? If you could have heard her talking to me today just before Philip came home, telling me how her heart is broken over her troubled marriage. How she wants to restore her relationship with Crew but is battling depression over her marriage. She is seeking the Lord for the first time in her life. Can't you all give her a break?"

Mary then shifted the conversation toward her mother.

"When you showed up at her house, all high and mighty, she said it made her feel like you believed her to be unworthy of God's love. How could you do that to a person you know is lost?"

"Don't try to put the guilt trip on me, because you know full well it's a waste of your time." Mary's mother wasn't about to back down. "This woman is obviously a masterful manipulator and is going to great lengths to seduce your husband and break up your marriage. Am I to gather from this hissy fit that you are taking Bonnie's side over your husband and *me*?"

Mary took a few seconds to consider her response. She needed no more time than that. She looked at Philip, whom she had loved most of her life. In all the years she'd known him, he had never lied to her or let her down. She then thought about her mother, who was quite a pistol but always trustworthy and honest.

"I'm saying I believe in what I saw. And today, I saw a humble woman wearing sneakers and a T-shirt, not a short, red dress with high heels. I don't know if you all are making these stories up because you are so paranoid about Bonnie and afraid she's going to hurt me or Crew...I don't know what it is. I may be the only person who believes in Bonnie, and it may make you all furious at me, but I believe her."

Chapter 29

"She's been bamboozled, Pops!" GiGi just couldn't believe it. The ride home from Mary and Philip's house was a long one. Poppy, GiGi, and Viv didn't dare leave until Wills returned with Tate and Crew; they did their level best to persuade Mary to consider the alternate scenario. But she wouldn't budge.

"Mary has dug her heels deep into the Tennessee red clay on this one. And, buddy, things are in a shambles," added Viv.

"You mean she's not going to budge until Bonnie catches Philip in her trap and ruins his reputation?" Poppy asked the two women rhetorically.

But GiGi responded anyway: "Dagnabit! This is a full-blown fiasco! You're right, Pops...that blond demon is gonna destroy Philip's reputation while Mary stands by and lets her."

"Stands by? Are you kidding? She's becoming the blond demon's accomplice." Viv's voice was sharp.

GiGi replied by mocking Mary: "I'm Mary, and I believe the she-devil's story over my husband. Go ahead, seductress, stop by my husband's office anytime you want...because I trust you!" She paused for just a moment, and the car went silent until she shot back one final exclamation: "Bonnie is a flasher, for crying out loud! No one can trust a flasher with their husband! This is way worse than the porno. God help us all!"

At the same time, back at the Montgomery home, Crew was gathering his backpack, preparing to head home for the evening. Calculating the best way to bring up a sticky subject with the fair-haired teenager, Philip spoke up: "Hey, do you mind if I walk you out to your car? I want to talk to you about something."

Crew was more than fine with it. The Montgomery family had become just that to him. Family.

Nightfall had settled in. Stars dotted the sky, and a slight chill drowned out the vestiges of the sun's heat. Old homes standing stately in a row down the expanse of the street were still awake, lights reflecting from the grand windows like a scene from *Gone with the Wind*.

"It's a beautiful night, isn't it?" Philip asked.

Crew couldn't help but wonder what Philip needed to talk to him about. "Yeah, it sure is," he answered.

"Crew, I'm not going to beat around the bush with you. I need to ask you a personal question, and I want you to trust me enough to give me a straight answer. You think you can do that for me?" he asked.

The boy's stomach filled with butterflies as he anticipated Philip's question. Being the cool, surfacy kid was easy for him; heartfelt, honest conversations were not.

"I'll try; what's up?" he returned.

"It's about your mother. She has started to show up at church, eating lunch after the service with Preacher and Jeannie, and now she's showing up at my house. I'm just curious about this sudden change in her. What do you think about it?"

Philip knew he was treading on sensitive territory. He thought of the resentment he would have if another adult asked his children the same kind of question, but he had to know.

"I don't really like to talk about my parents." Crew mumbled the words, running his fingers through his hair. "My relationship with them is so messed up."

Philip kept digging: "So your relationship with your mom is still messed up? I'm confused about that. She seems to be making more of an effort with you."

"My relationship with my mom is screwed up." Crew dropped his backpack on the ground, deciding to open up a little. "What you're really wanting to know is whether I'm still being locked up in the basement, right?"

Philip saw the pain when he looked into the boy's eyes. Crew had become a master at covering it all up with his good looks and charm, but tonight, the pain was evident.

"It's embarrassing for me to talk about or to even think about, but yes, I am still living in basement hell." He made an effort to jokingly laugh it off but failed. "I don't get it, Mr. Montgomery. The only time she acknowledges my existence is when she shows up at church. And tonight, her showing up here...wow." He rubbed his fingers through his blond hair again. "Well, it's like she's crossed into Crazy Blonde Town or something."

Philip wished he could unload about Bonnie's advances on him but knew he couldn't. "How about your dad? Where does that relationship fit into all of this mess?"

Crew shoved his hand down deep into his pocket and pulled out a cell phone. Holding it out toward Philip, he became brutally honest: "He fits right about here. I haven't seen him in months, but he sends his obligatory texts to me almost every day so I'll know he's thinking of me...what a laugh, right? I'm sure he's found a new girlfriend who is occupying whatever time he's not spending being a workaholic. It's just the way things are. I've accepted it."

"So you think your parents will divorce?" Philip didn't let up.

"Divorce?" Crew was genuinely surprised by the question. "You really don't know my mother at all, do you? My father couldn't divorce her if he tried.

She has way too much dirt on him; she would bury him. No, my dad has money. Lots of it. And he pays Mom a hefty sum to keep the dirt to herself." Crew looked off into the distance, in the direction of his home. "Make no mistake about it, sir. My mom controls my dad like a puppet. It's not the other way around. She loves her life exactly the way it is, so nothing is going to change anytime soon."

Philip had heard plenty. He didn't want or need any other information. "Crew, I am so sorry. I mean that, son. And I'm glad the Lord chose to place you into our lives. I don't understand what's going on with your parents, and I don't need to understand, because I know Who our Heavenly Father is...and I know He loves everything about you. He's always with you, like I've told you before; He's even in that basement with you at night...and we are always here for you too. You can count on us."

Philip gave the teenager a pat on his back before bringing him in close for a hug.

"Mr. Montgomery?" Crew asked. "I'm thinking about being baptized, and I was hoping you'd stand up there with me since my dad won't be there."

"I'd be honored. And I'll be happy to let the whole church know the change I've seen in your life because of Jesus. He is going to do mighty things in your life, Crew."

Crew's reply was barely audible...just a whisper: "He already is."

Chapter 30

Crew could hardly wait to tell Preacher Walker and Jeannie the good news. He'd finally found the courage to ask Philip to stand as a witness for him during his baptism, and Philip had been genuinely happy about it. The next date for baptisms was only one month away. Crew's calendar was marked to signify the beginning of a new chapter in his life.

Mary reached out more and more to Bonnie during the weeks leading up to the baptism, even inviting her over each morning to do Bible study with her. Bonnie, eager to drive a wedge between Mary and Philip, never turned down a single invitation. Her obsessive-compulsive nature was now laser focused on destroying Mary. Pretending to be interested in church, the Bible, and Jesus, Bonnie memorized scripture and led prayers to impress her adversary. She even thought to return a couple of the items she'd stolen, Mary's Bible and Miss Charity's princess crown, stealthily sneaking them into the house to be found by an unsuspecting Mary, who was eager to prove that members of her family were wrong about Bonnie. Mary, bent on proselytizing her lost friend, was as oblivious as ever.

As for Philip, he did his best to avoid the blond bombshell, which became more difficult, near impossible, by the day. Every time Mary turned her head, Bonnie would cast Philip a seductive look and touch her breasts or lift her skirt to tease him. She was a master at the tease. Philip continually asked himself if she was doing it on purpose or if all her actions were completely innocent. Bonnie was fully aware, plotting every move, knowing she had him exactly where she wanted him.

Compared to Mary, who was typically dressed in yoga pants, a T-shirt, and flip-flops, Bonnie always made sure to dress frisky and provocative. Her clothing, if it was sending a message, shouted, "Come and get me!" It was fruitless for Philip to report the behavior to Mary, because she had already proven she wouldn't believe him. So, his faithful confidants were his in-laws and Preacher Walker. What they didn't know, however, was the inner struggle going on inside Philip. He had grown accustomed to Bonnie's attention and began to look forward to her visits to his home each morning. He secretly fantasized about her making another surprise visit to his office, but the visit in his imagination ended much differently than the first.

Slowly but surely, Bonnie chipped away at the protective covering around the Montgomery marriage. On Sunday mornings, when Mary was busy tending to Miss Charity and visiting with other members of the church, she made time to ask him about his week, to compliment him on the way he was dressed, or to question him about a particular point in scripture. She made him feel important.

Noticed. Masculine. He took note of how Bonnie had a keen sense of knowing what to say and how to say it, and he found her to be thoughtful. Unlike Mary, she took time to appreciate him.

Philip mowed his lawn and clipped hedges on Saturday mornings before lunch, and Bonnie, who had applied his routine to her memory, always stopped for a prearranged visit with Mary, which typically began with a ten- or fifteen-minute conversation outside with Philip in the front yard.

A month had passed, and the following day was Crew's baptism.

"How is it that I always find you mowing your yard on Saturday mornings, Philip Montgomery?" she asked, pretending to be in a hurry. "I swear, Mary better appreciate the hardworking man she is so lucky to be married to."

Philip teased, "You know she takes me for granted; everybody takes me for granted."

"Except me," Bonnie answered with a flirty grin.

She was wearing daisy duke cutoff jeans, a plunging white V-neck blouse, and a pair of stacked sandals. The scent of something mysteriously musky floated all around her, providing a sharp contrast to the smell of freshly cut grass.

"Is Crew ready for his baptism tomorrow?" He quickly changed the subject.

"Oh, I don't know...well, I wouldn't know...because he won't talk to me," Bonnie returned sorrowfully.

Philip, taking advantage of the opportunity that presented itself, continued: "Can I talk with you about something very frank? I mean, I believe we've developed a sort of friendship over the last several weeks, and friends can talk openly, right?"

"Sure. I love to talk to you and always want to know what you think about everything. You are so smart."

Flattery got Bonnie everything she'd always wanted. Philip wouldn't be able to resist her for very much longer.

"I've got a real special relationship with Crew, you know, and he tells me you force him to stay in the basement, away from the main house. And if that's true, well, I can see why your relationship with him might be strained."

Bonnie shook her head. "Is that what he's told you? That I lock him in the basement? I'm shocked...and sad too. This is hurtful," she pouted.

No one was more shocked than Philip. He had believed Crew's story since the moment he heard it. "You mean you don't lock him out of your main house?"

"Well, I've locked the door, but not without telling him first. I hate to admit this to you, since you are such a fine Christian man and all, but there was a time not too long ago when I was a very naughty woman. I didn't know any better because I didn't have a relationship with God like I do now, you know what I mean? Anyway, I'd have a man over every once in a while...and...well, things happened that Crew didn't need to see." Putting her hands on both cheeks as if getting ready to give Philip some earth-shattering news, she whispered: "I think I may have an addiction to sex...I'm really frisky in the bedroom."

Philip could've stopped the conversation right there. And as a married man, he should have. But instead, he encouraged her to go on by saying nothing. Bonnie continued: "So yeah, I'd tell him I was having a friend over and would be locking the door. But that was it. It never stayed locked all the time and hasn't been locked at all since I started going to church. The door thing worked both ways. There were plenty of times he would have a party or a girl over and would tell me not to come in the basement and interrupt his good time. We had a mutual respect for one another until recently, when he turned away from me completely."

"I'm confused then," he answered, trying to get the whole "I may have an addiction to sex" comment off his brain. "Why the sudden change between you and Crew? Church should have brought you two closer together instead of pulling you apart."

Bonnie held an invisible fishing line; her words dangled like a cricket in an open body of water. She'd captured countless men in her past this way.

"I think he's angry that his father left us. I don't know how much you know about that situation, but we are married in name only. It's been that way for a very long time. Crew blames me; I'm sure of it, but there was nothing I could do. His father left me and has lived with his mistress in Chattanooga for the last couple of years."

As Bonnie began to cry, Philip instinctively reached out, pulled her to him, and held her in his arms.

"I'm so sorry I've made you cry; I didn't know," he said, petting the back of her hair with his hand.

"It's been difficult, but I'm doing better now that I've found the Lord...and now that I've found you...and Mary." She pressed her body close to Philip's. "I'm thankful Crew has you as a father figure. That's all that matters to me right now. He'll come around and love me again at some point. I'm certain of it." Tears continued to flow, because Bonnie knew Philip would hold her until the last tear drop was wiped away.

"Is there anything I can do?" he asked.

"I'd hate to ask it. You and Mary have done so much for me and Crew already. You all are like family to us both," she answered.

"No, please ask. I want to help. I love Crew and have grown so fond of you, Bonnie. If there is anything I can do to help, just name it."

Bonnie decided it was time to jerk her fishing line tight. "Well, if you're sure. And if you'll feel free to tell me no if I'm asking something that is way too much for you." She pulled back, still holding Philip, and looked up into his eyes. "Do you promise?"

Philip became lost in the embrace and in her blue eyes. "Of course I promise. Tell me what you're thinking."

Realizing he was standing in his front yard holding a woman who was clearly not his wife, Philip let Bonnie go. The embrace came to an abrupt end, but he was hooked, so it didn't matter.

"I'd like for you to counsel me." Bonnie's voice became happy and cheerful at the thought of it. "Mary has included me in her Bible-study time each morning, and I am learning so much about the Bible and about how to be a godly woman. But I think I could use your counsel too. As a man who is an incredible father, you could teach me how to be both a mother and a father to my son. You know more about teenage boys than I could ever possibly learn on my own. After Crew gets baptized tomorrow, I want to have a new start with him. I'd only need about three or four weeks. What do you think? Have I asked too much?"

Bonnie knew she hadn't asked too much. She'd planned her pursuit out perfectly. If she'd asked for six months, that would've been too much. But what harm would three or four weeks produce, really? *C'mon, Philip, you know you're going to say yes...just say it*, she thought.

"Let me talk it over with Mary," he answered.

"I have asked too much. I've probably overstepped a boundary, huh? Please forgive me, Philip; I am so new to this whole Christian thing. Of course you probably don't think it is appropriate to counsel a woman. What would people think about an upstanding church leader like you giving counsel to a woman who has a reputation like me? Don't ask Mary. Let's just pretend I never asked the question."

Philip hated to offend Bonnie. Truthfully, the fact that he hated to hurt the feelings of others was one of his greatest weaknesses. And it was about to get him into trouble.

"No, Bonnie, you have not asked too much. I don't have to talk to Mary about it at all. She has been eager for our family to come alongside you on this journey of faith and has encouraged me to have a friendship with you. I think my giving you some pointers on how to build a better relationship with Crew would please her, so let's just plan on it. When do you want to begin your sessions with Counselor Montgomery?" he teased.

"Philip," she responded, "you always know how to make me feel good. I was thinking I could come by your office just after closing on Tuesdays for the next few weeks. Could you spare thirty minutes a week, or is that going to cut into your family time too much?"

Bonnie's request seemed legitimate and reasonable. Philip, without further consideration, made her day: "Tuesdays it is. Let's begin this week!"

Just as Bonnie was beginning to make her way up to the front porch, Mary stepped out.

"Hey, Bonnie, I thought it was about time for you to get here! Are you ready for some coffee and girl time?" she asked, genuinely happy to see her new friend.

Bonnie was quick to seal her deal: "Yes, of course I am, and I have some great news! I have just convinced your husband to give me some pointers on how to build my relationship with Crew. He's agreed for me to meet him for a few thirty-minute sessions on Tuesdays after he closes the office."

"That's really sweet of you, Chief," Mary beamed. "Why don't you do the sessions here? Then Bonnie can plan to stay for dinner!"

Bonnie already had an answer: "No, Mary, that won't work, since Crew will be here. You know he eats dinner with you guys every evening now. I don't want him to know about this at all...it has to remain our secret, all right?"

Mary walked down the steps to stand beside Bonnie, both women facing Philip. "You're right; Crew doesn't need to know about this at all. Philip, where do you suggest the meeting take place?" she asked.

Before Philip could respond, Bonnie jumped in: "I could stop by Philip's office, and we could do the sessions there."

Mary hesitated. She didn't know why, but the thought of Bonnie and Philip alone in his office didn't settle well with her spirit. But the uneasy feeling left as quickly as it had come, so Mary decided she was just being a silly, overprotective wife. "That would be perfect!"

It was settled. Tuesdays were now Bonnie's favorite day of the week.

Chapter 31

Sunday was a complete blur to Philip. Crew's baptism, as far as he could recall, went off without a hitch. But for the life of him, he couldn't remember a single word Preacher Walker spoke.

"Are you all right, Philip?" the pastor asked once the service was over.

Philip was used to sharing honestly with his mentor, but he was too ashamed to speak about his attraction to Bonnie. "Oh, yeah, I'm fine...just not feeling too well today."

"Well, I sure do hope you feel like partaking of the feast today. You know, I believe every member of the church brought a dish for our big luncheon to celebrate the baptisms today. There is nothin' quite like southern cooking, is there?"

Philip walked away as the preacher was finishing the question. *Lord*, the elder gentleman silently prayed, *I don't know what's going on with Philip, but shower him with Your blessings today.*

Bonnie, who was not a cook, showed up with two huge pans of banana pudding, claiming it was her grandmother's recipe. No one believed her. Her figure was too perfect to be one that had ever allowed banana pudding to touch her lips.

GiGi decided to test her: "I'm a big banana pudding fan, Bonnie, but I don't believe I've ever tasted a pudding quite as good as you have made today."

Knowing it was probably a trap, the blond demon tried to make an escape, but she found herself surrounded by other women of the church who were eager to agree with GiGi's assessment.

"What is your recipe, sweetheart?" GiGi continued, hiding her venom.

Bonnie, who'd purchased the banana pudding from an out-of-the-way baker in Chattanooga, managed to squirm out of the question. "Now, you should know this rule as well as anyone around here, since you are a Southern hell...oops, I meant a Southern belle...excuse me, ladies; all that talking the preacher did about hell today caused me to slip up, I guess." She giggled, acting out a faint hint of shame. "As I was saying," she went on, drawing in her small audience, who appeared to dismiss the "Southern hell" comment, "a real southerner never gives out her secret recipes."

Bonnie walked away with a slight wave while simultaneously shooting GiGi the look of a big, fat *Ha!*

The elder woman watched the blonde work the room, but she was most concerned by the way her eyes consistently fell upon Philip. At one point, she watched Bonnie pull Philip over to the table that held her now-infamous banana pudding. Although she couldn't make out the conversation by reading their lips, she read their body language loud and clear. Things were getting out of hand.

"Philip," Bonnie urged, "come try my banana pudding. Mary told me it is your favorite dessert, so I made it especially for you, since you were so sweet to stand with Crew today while he was baptized."

What could the man say or do? He was at a church luncheon and couldn't be rude. After taking a bite, his face lit up like the moon over the ocean on a summer's night; indeed, it was the best banana pudding he'd ever tasted. "This is wonderful, Bonnie. I think I could eat that whole pan and still want more."

"Oh my gosh, I am thrilled you like it. Do you remember the other day when I told you I can be sort of a bad girl in the bedroom?" she giggled.

Philip didn't answer. He just kept plowing his face full of the pudding, wondering where Bonnie was going to go with the conversation.

"Well, the last time I made banana pudding, I was a very bad girl...a very, very bad girl."

She let the words hang there with him. A few parishioners came up to the table, helping themselves to some banana pudding and other desserts. Bonnie and Philip were cordial to them, offering a word or two, but neither moved away from the table. When everyone had walked away, leaving the two alone again, Bonnie continued: "Do you want me to tell you what I did? It's quite funny, given the fact that you are eating the pudding right now. I won't give you all the details, just enough for you to get the general idea." She laughed, making the whole exchange seem as innocent as child's play.

Philip, mouth halfway full, managed a "Sure, why not?" Inside, he wanted every detail and hated himself for feeling that way.

"Let's just say I surprised my date with banana pudding, but it was served on a place setting of Bonnie Cutless instead of an aluminum pan." She reached down with her index finger, which was embellished with a long, red fingernail, and pulled up a taste of banana pudding, brought it to her mouth, and used her tongue to remove it. "It was a really fun night." She blew him a kiss before walking away, leaving the vivid picture in Philip's mind.

GiGi watched intently, seeing Philip's eyes lingering on Bonnie as she moved away from him and the banana pudding. A foreboding feeling came upon her. For the first time, she realized Bonnie's trap was actually working.

"Mary, you better wake up." She found her daughter quickly, giving her a rundown on what she'd just witnessed.

Mary, holding a very hyperactive Miss Charity, who had been given too many cookies by well-meaning church folk, didn't have the energy to listen.

"Mom, Philip and I are on the same page with Bonnie...please, let it go."

"On the same page?" She didn't give up. "You're not even in the same book! You'll find Bonnie's page-turner, by the way, in the adult smut section. It's entitled *How I Stole Mary Montgomery's Husband out from under Her Own Nose!*" Mary tried to walk away, but GiGi followed her. "She is after your husband, and to be honest, Philip is starting to look at her in a different way. I think he's attracted to her."

"And he's now going to leave me for Bonnie's banana pudding...isn't that what you're saying?" Ridicule rolled off her daughter's tongue. "You really think they are making eyes at one another at the dessert table during a church potluck luncheon on the grounds? Please tell me you hear how absurd you sound!" Mary turned toward her mother, pushed the little Miss into her arms, and said, "Since you seem to have so much energy and an excessive amount of idle time, take your granddaughter for a while and focus on her. I really don't want to talk about Bonnie ever again unless it is in a positive way."

She walked away, leaving GiGi with her squirmy granddaughter. Miss Charity threw her arms around her grandma's neck and pulled her in for a close hug.

"That's right; hug me tight, little one, because a big storm is a-comin'...or an earthquake...or maybe a full-on tidal wave...and she's wearing a dress that looks like it's been painted on. God help us all."

Later that evening, when the kids were already tucked in bed, Mary was surprised to hear a tap at the front door. Already dressed in her nightgown, propped up in bed, and reading a book, she asked Philip to check it out.

"I didn't hear anything," he told her. But being the ever-dutiful husband, he halfheartedly obliged. His bare feet padded the wood floor softly, careful not to wake the sleeping children. Peeking out the front window, he saw Bonnie standing in her knee-length bathrobe at his front door holding an aluminum pan. Her hair was pulled up into a sloppy knot on her head with long pieces of blond waves hanging down to frame her face. She was a vision.

Philip clicked on the front-porch light and opened the door. "What brings you here this time of night?"

"I know it's late, but I couldn't sleep. I just kept lying there in my bed thinking about Crew's baptism and the excitement surrounding the day. All my thoughts kept coming back to you and the kindness you continue to show my son and me. I just had to tell you thank you again, and I thought the best way to do it was to bring over what was left of the banana pudding. Now that I'm here, I feel sort of silly."

Philip quickly chimed in: "Don't feel silly at all. I'll take that banana pudding off your hands any time of day or night. Honestly, it is the best I've ever tasted." He took the aluminum pan and stood waiting for Bonnie to excuse herself for the night.

"Maybe you can have a midnight snack or something." She acted shy, figuring he would be drawn to reassure her.

Philip didn't disappoint. "A midnight snack sounds amazing."

"I'm so glad we are neighbors, Philip. And I'm looking forward to spending Tuesdays with you. Can you believe Crew let me give him a hug today? That's progress, right?" she asked.

"It's all about taking it one step at a time. He'll come around. I don't know if I'll be able to offer any magical advice to you, but I will enjoy trying to help out. Crew needs to have a relationship with you. You're a good momma, Bonnie; you love your son...that's the secret ingredient. Let him know you love him." Philip felt awkward standing there in the doorway without a shirt, wearing only a pair of checked pajama pants. Was she checking him out, he wondered? It certainly looked like it.

"Well, I better get back to the house. Like I said, I just wanted to say thank you for being a part of one of the most important days of Crew's life. I know he'll never forget it." She began to walk away but made a split-second decision to load an invisible cricket on her line and throw it out again without caution into the dark water. "I think this is the first time I've ever seen you without a shirt, and I like it. Don't eat too much of that banana pudding, or you might get a pot belly and ruin that sexy six-pack."

Philip took the bait. "What? Are you flirting with me?"

"Me? Flirt with you?" She gave him a giggle, tucked a wispy tendril behind her ear, and turned to make her way back home. Philip, unmoving, stood and watched her. As she made her way off the final step, knowing Philip's eyes were fixated on her backside, she gave him a quick glance. "If you weren't a married man, I'd do so much more than flirt with you."

From that second forward, it was official. Philip wanted Bonnie.

"What took you so long?" was all Mary asked when Philip finally returned to their bedroom.

"It was Bonnie. She couldn't sleep because she was thinking about the baptism and the luncheon, so she brought over the last of the banana pudding thinking we might want to have a midnight snack," he answered.

Mary put down her book and grinned. "She is so sweet, isn't she? I didn't get a taste of that pudding today, and think I'd love to have a midnight snack; how about you?"

The two were standing in the kitchen, each with a fork, digging into the aluminum pan together. "My mother told me today that you're going to leave me for Bonnie and her banana pudding. She said she saw you guys 'making eyes' with one another today around the dessert table. Tsk. Tsk. Tsk. Philip," Mary joked.

Philip didn't laugh.

"She said what?" he asked, slightly perturbed by the revelation.

"Oh, you know my momma...she's always thinking the worst about every situation. To her, I think, life is a soap opera, and her family has the starring role."

Philip thought about what he should say next. His heart was beating fast as he considered how he and Bonnie were being watched by Mary's mother, the snoop. What had she seen? And had she heard any of their conversation?

"Is that all she said?"

"Other than saying you are showing signs of being attracted to Bonnie and how blind as a bat I am...umm, no, that pretty much covers it." Mary laughed out loud; Philip joined in and laughed along with her.

Philip didn't sleep a whole lot that night. Instead of considering how he could avoid an affair with Bonnie, he began to plot how he could be with her and not get caught. As for the blond bombshell, she drifted off to sleep after her toes swished the crisp sheets for the one hundredth time. Lying still, she sang aloud: "Mary had a handsome man, handsome man, handsome man...Mary had a handsome man 'til Bonnie stole him away. Now Mary is so very sad, very sad, very sad...now Mary is so very sad...what's wrong, dear; don't you like to play?"

Bonnie laughed out loud. Crew, locked in the basement, heard the distant sound of her cackling as he knelt beside his bed finishing up his prayers.

"Lord, I don't know what's up with my crazy mother. Please protect Mary and Philip from anything she might do to hurt them. She's up to something; I know she is..."

Two angels were standing guard in his room. One said to the other: "That GiGi sure is a bird, ain't she?"

The other replied: "Yep, she called it today...a big storm is a-comin'."

Author's Note

This book is the first in a series of books that will follow the Montgomery family. The name of the series, Loyalty Lock, denotes the common denominator running through each life represented. My teenage daughter, Lydia, created unique tokens for fans of this series that can be purchased for $10.00 by contacting me at melaniekhollis@gmail.com while supplies last. Funds raised through the sale of the Loyalty Lock tokens will go to support the special-needs community.

Acknowledgments

I'm afraid to try to list the names of all the friends and family members who have supported me in this endeavor for fear of accidentally leaving someone out and hurting feelings, so I'll simply say a huge thank-you and send hugs. You all know who you are, and I appreciate you more than I can express.

To GiGi: it is so much fun having a "nutjob" as a mom...so glad you could come along and become the star of my book, because you are forever a star in my life!

To Hope and Charlie, the little specials in my life: this book wouldn't have been written if it weren't for you. I am so happy God perfectly created you to be everything you are, and even happier that He chose to place you in my life. I am beyond blessed and am mindful of that fact every day when I get to hold you in my arms.

To Preacher Walker and Jeannie: You have shaped my life in so many ways, and my heart is filled to the brim with love and appreciation for you.

To Grandad and Grandmomma: I miss you terribly and look forward to our reunion in glory when Grandmomma will *run* to greet me...no more wheelchair!

And to my Lydia, who relentlessly stood alongside me daily as I wrestled through this book for nearly six months: you are the best for more reasons than I can count. The way you love Hope and Charlie, unselfishly and unconditionally, blows me away...my little minion (insert winky face)!

www.ingramcontent.com/pod-product-compliance
Lightning Source LLC
Chambersburg PA
CBHW071132170626
46809CB00002B/591